Bluetooth
& the World Wide Web

To Milo

'Bluetooth & the World Wide Web'

Written & Edited by E. Rachael Hardcastle

Created by David Hardcastle.

Curious Cat Books, United Kingdom

Printed by Ingramspark

For permissions contact the author/s via:

www.erachaelhardcastle.com

Illustrations by Christine Martin.

E-Book Available

ISBN: 978-1-9999688-3-0

First Edition

Bluetooth & the World Wide Web

Created by David Hardcastle
Written by E. Rachael Hardcastle
Illustrated by Christine Martin

In association with ScHnELL Custom Snail Shop.

This book is <u>TOP SECRET</u> and will self-destruct in 5...4...3...2...1...

OK, not really, but wouldn't that be AWESOME?

Acknowledgements

This book started as one of my dad's wacky story ideas, which he shared with me one morning over coffee. I wasn't sure at first because I hadn't written a children's book before. However, after a few days (plus more coffee, biscuits and a longer discussion) we decided to co-write *Bluetooth & the World Wide Web* to entertain families all over the world at bed time.

My grandad, Peter (aka 'Big Pete') and my grandma, Janet often read to me when I visited their home in West Yorkshire, and those happy memories are still with me to this day. Not only did this help me learn to read and write (particularly to improve my spelling, I remember reading the dictionary with Big Pete), but I got to explore some amazing fictional worlds, guided by two of my favourite people. Mobile phones and video games just cannot compare.

For this reason, our book is, of course, in loving memory of my grandparents.

But when I lost my grandad in 2003, my great uncle Fred (aka Fleadrick Pond) and aunt Avril stepped in to offer their support after school. Their encouragement and the fun times we spent together have also contributed to who I am today. And as I write this at Easter time, I'm reminded of past springs with Fred and Avril, checking to see if their Easter chicken had visited, then sitting on a little stool in the living room to eat my boiled egg with buttered soldiers.

This book is also with thanks to, and in loving memory of, my aunt and uncle.

I'd like to thank my parents too for their support and for always cheering me on—motivating me on my writing and business adventures and never failing to believe in my future success (even when I don't!).

From the cover of this book you'll already know I co-wrote *Bluetooth & the World Wide Web* with its creator, my dad, David Hardcastle. Without his input it would never have been as wacky, as funny or as imaginative (*believe me!*), so if you enjoy what you're about to read, credit goes to my dad.

All authors know, though, that writing a book (although a solitary hobby at its core) involves tons of other people, all of whom I'd like to thank now.

To my mum, Dawn and my partner, Sam for putting up with our many 'working' lunches and busy weekends, the sudden changes of subject (to talk about Bluetooth... *again*) and for their help and positivity, even when things went wrong.

To all our volunteer mascots and BETA readers, who sacrificed their time to proofread a manuscript or promote a signing.

To Tony, our inspiration for Alfrid Jennings.

To our fabulous (and extremely talented) illustrator, Christine for bringing Bluetooth and his friends to life.

And, finally, to all the retailers and readers out there who are buying, stocking, sharing and reading Bluetooth's story. Thank you! Independent authors really do value all their readers—we do this for you, and we're grateful (always) for your support.

From our family to yours, with love.

David and E. Rachael Hardcastle

Chapter One

It was Simon Ranchilla's turn to read aloud from the textbook, and his bossy history teacher Mrs Longlegs was awaiting his first nervous words at the front of the class.

Simon had been staring at the pages of *The History of the World Wide Web* now for at least ten minutes without a sound. Every time he opened his mouth to speak, the hairs on all eight of his spindly legs stood on end, and he'd swallowed hard to fight the sickness in his stomach. He had awful fang ache too, which seemed to happen when Simon was under pressure. Just last week, he'd been reading from an older book about the function of the Hyper Touch Transfer Protocol (or the HTTP), when two mischievous grasshoppers at the back of the class started sniggering. His fang had *really* ached then!

After that, Simon retreated behind the pages of his textbook and followed along silently with everyone else, learning about the HTTP's vibration speeds along the Web. If the bullies couldn't hear his voice, they couldn't pick on him for how underdeveloped and squeaky it was for his age.

Mrs Longlegs hadn't singled Simon out on purpose though, and like his friends, she too called him by his nickname, Bluetooth (but not in front of the other children). Despite her strict nature and the way she narrowed all eight of her beady eyes at you over her bottle bottom eyeglass, she was very understanding of his shy personality, so he took the name lightly. For an older and better-educated spider, Mrs Longlegs wasn't so intimidating in appearance because most of her hair had thinned and she'd shrunken over the years. Simon noted, however, that she, too, was *still* taller than him. While other insects in the class gasped when she glared at them through the bottom half of her eyeglass—her eyes suddenly seeming ENORMOUS—Simon thought it rather comical.

But he knew it was only fair and important for him to participate like the other insects in his class, and her encouragement was for his own good. Reading aloud today, though, as the boys waited in anticipation for another reason to poke fun at him or use his beloved nickname against him was, so far, the most terrifying moment of Simon's childhood.

"The World Wide Web (or the WWW) has existed for millions of years," Simon began in a whisper.

He was immediately prompted by Mrs Longlegs to, 'Please speak up, Dear', as she gave him a reassuring pat on the back.

Simon cleared his throat and, aware of how distracting his lisp was (given how he hadn't yet grown into his only fang—a single aqua blue eyesore), he anxiously continued.

"Before humans adapted it for their own purpose and benefit, the Web belonged exclusively to spiders, who used it to communicate with, and on behalf of, the insect world," he said. "Spinning an intricate silk web is harder than it looks; it takes patience and practice to ensure each thread is the ideal length and thickness to do the job. It must be strong enough to take every twang of code, no matter the HTTP vibration speed, and perfectly translucent to hide it from Web Attack Special Patrol (or WASP) swarms."

Simon paused and looked up, then instantly regretted it. The grasshoppers were whispering again and laughing, sending their own messages through the silk strings connecting their wooden desks to the class Web, which covered the ceiling above them. Simon had no doubt those messages would be transferred to his own desk; something cruel and degrading to look forward to when Mrs Longlegs finally excused him from the spotlight. He winced as another sharp pain pulsed through his blue fang.

"And what do the swarms do?" Mrs Longlegs prompted.

In unison, the class chanted, "*Hack the Web!*"

"That's right. They hack the Web; sever the connections and use their sharp stingers to slash and inject *what* into the system?"

"*Virus vibrations,*" the class replied.

"And, as we know from page thirteen, those viruses send fake messages and news across the World Wide Web to cause chaos. That's why the government created the MicrobeSift Department of Security," she said. "Simon, please continue from page thirteen."

Simon gripped his textbook a little harder and said, "The MicrobeSift workers were introduced into the system approximately fifty years ago to filter these viruses, preparing the existing silk to be salvaged and repaired with stronger hashtag patches by spiders."

"Very good. Thank you, Simon. You may sit down now."

Only when he was safely in his seat again could he exhale and settle the trembling in his legs. But not for long. As he predicted, the silk connecting the class Web to his personal webbook was now jiggling, indicating he had an unread eco-mail from Diddit and Ranoff, the two grasshopper bullies.

"Don't forget, there's a test this week on the creation and purpose of the World Wide Web, and there will be a quiz tomorrow about the start of the Great Feud. I expect you *all* to study hard. Class dismissed."

Simon shook his head and slammed the lid of his webbook closed, then quickly disconnected it from the class Web above. He'd reconnect to his home Web later, and until then the unread message would become just another of his pointless fears.

Simon rummaged in his locker for another twenty minutes. He figured the longer he lingered in the halls looking busy, the less likely he was to bump into the bullies Diddit and Ranoff on their way out. Only when the halls were eerily quiet did he set off with his friends, hoping to be back at his home in the Old Barn in time for supper.

Dot and Dash Spinn (nicknamed by Simon as the Binary Twins for their love of technology) were the school's only identical spiders and Simon's most loyal friends. Their mother Claire Spinn had been attending a spin class with Mrs Ranchilla since he could remember.

Simon was in awe of Claire Spinn because she was a HUGE deal in the spider (and computer nerd) community. Although the Spinn family was among the richest and best known in the community, Dot and Dash similarly struggled when it came to bullies, bringing the trio closer. But, despite the peer pressure to be popular and sporty, it was Mrs Spinn who inspired the friends to learn to code instead. Her kids did nothing else in their spare time and had created their own private means to pass secret notes in class.

Mrs Longlegs hadn't yet caught on to the coded messaging system they were calling 'Binary', but Simon knew it would only be a matter of time.

Claire Spinn had been the first spider to develop the electronic webbook, an earlier model of that the students were currently using in school, and the Spinn company was in the process of advancing the Web's communication systems with a fun new social media project called

'Scuttle Bugg'. Simon and the twins couldn't wait to bug test it for her!

It was almost dark in the streets now, and the horizon's fading glow guided them back toward the Old Barn. They followed the shadows cast across the pavement, picking up the pace as the temperature dropped and they began to see puffs of their icy breath.

Dash skipped along the pavement, flicking droplets of puddle water back at his sister, Dorothy. It was definitely sweater and scarf weather, and they were lucky it wasn't snowing yet. Spiders always struggled to navigate a safe path home in the snow despite wearing two or three pairs of winter boots; too many legs, too many obstacles.

"Is Scuttle Bugg ready for us to play with yet?" Simon asked Dash.

"Not yet, but we can show you some of the cool features when we reconnect to your home Web," he replied. "Mum gave me the BETA disc."

"I can't believe your mum is letting you sleep over," said Simon, excitedly.

"I know and on a school night!" said Dorothy, scurrying to keep up with the boys. "Hey, what's for supper?"

"Fast food." Simon licked his lips, careful to avoid the sharp point of his single blue fang. "Think she's ordering from McFly's."

Dash pulled a face and stuck out his tongue. "Ugh, they were so slow to deliver last time, though. We were waiting for ages! Why do they have to use *snails?* They're useless and ugly."

"They have as much right to work as anyone else, Dash," said his sister, "and if you're going to be snailest then I'm telling mum!"

"Dot, don't be such a tattle tail! I'm not snailest, I'm realistic. Bluetooth agrees with me, don't you?"

Simon shrugged and kicked a pebble. He was still worried about that unread eco-mail. After reconnecting to his home Web, the Binary Twins would insist on telling Simon's mum about the hurtful eco-mails he'd been receiving, and she'd want to speak to the Head.

Anything but that, he thought.

Already his tooth was aching. He didn't need a headache too!

"I dunno," he said after a long pause, "it's not *their* fault your mum's company made their jobs redundant. Nobody uses Snail Mail anymore, not when they can send eco-mail."

"It's not her fault!" Dash argued.

"I never said it was," said Simon, "but have you ever even met a snail?"

"Of course I have! We still get Snail Mail every day. At least, we will until the end of the year. Dad says posting letters is bad for the environment anyway. He wants to go digital."

"It *is* bad for the environment," Dot agreed. "It's a waste of paper, but you just can't beat a hand-written love letter." She blushed, thinking about the anonymous card she'd received on Valentine's Day via Snail Mail, and how special it had made her feel. She sighed, "You stupid boys wouldn't understand."

Now it was Simon's turn to blush because he had secretly sent Dorothy that Valentine's card. So they wouldn't identify his handwriting, he'd even used one of his left legs to write a short, messy poem. It read:

'I love who you are,
I think you're so cute,
Smart as a bee,
Cute as newt.
But I think I'm more frog
than a bandy young bug,
A little bit odd
and in need of a hug.
So I'm making this plea,

To you sweet valentine,
Just once kiss this frog
and for ever be mine.'

"Hey, look!" Dash suddenly shouted. "Why are all the street lights out?"

Simon glanced up at the first post, then waved at the bored firefly sitting on it. "Hi, Dave!" he chirped. "Is everything OK?"

Dave the firefly jumped to attention and squeezed hard to illuminate his bottom. This temporarily highlighted the pavement like a spotlight on a blackened stage.

"Hi, Bluetooth. Sure, have you been to school today; studying hard?"

"Yes, we have a history test this week."

"Good lad, you hurry home now. Remember there's a curfew. Say hello to your mum for me!"

"See you later!" Simon turned to Dash and shrugged. "All looks OK to me."

"It's a blackout because of WASP," Dot said, pulling the Spider Twines newspaper from her satchel to show them the front page. "The fireflies are still on duty, but the swarms have been targeting street Webs in this area. We can't be out too late."

"Oh, I thought it was to save money or something," Dash said, grinning.

"No, I heard Mrs Longlegs talking to the Head about it today," Simon added.

The Head was the school's Headmaster, but the pupils (and most of the teachers) didn't know his real name. The Head was a borer grub worm, and he had a HUGE ROUND HEAD which balanced precariously on his long, wriggly body. Though he was usually a very patient worm, if he got really angry his mouth would open SO WIDE that you could see both rows of his over-sized teeth, then his teeny tiny eyes would pop out beneath rimless spectacles.

Simon waved at the next firefly along the road. "Hi, Lou, how are you?"

"Hi, Bluetooth. Same dung, different day. Your mum said you aced that quiz last week. Well done, Kid!"

Before Simon could thank him, they were interrupted by two young moths crossing the street, dressed in pink skirts and heels. They were gossiping about make-up and their crushes at school. Simon and his friends moved aside so they could pass, and had to wait a few minutes before finishing their conversations as the moths stopped to glare lovingly into the light.

"*Whoa*," they gasped mid-sentence. "*Preettty light!*"

E. Rachael Hardcastle & David Hardcastle

"Uhm, excuse me," said Dash. "Hey! I said *excuse* me!"

Simon sighed and called up to Lou. "Turn off the light!"

Lou grumbled, "Stop staring at my butt you two!"

The moths shook their heads when the light went out, blushed and giggled, then carried on walking as if nothing had happened. Lou illuminated the path again when they'd gone.

Simon shrugged. "I'll tell Mum you said hello!"

"Thanks, Bluetooth. Hurry along now, it's not safe," Lou yelled back, then extinguished his butt again.

The trio picked up the pace.

"Your mum knows a *lot* of fireflies," Dot said. "Are they friends?"

Simon nodded. "Mum knows tons of local bugs. She teaches aerobics at the community centre on Thursday nights."

"Any wasps?"

Simon scowled. "You're joking, right?"

"I don't get why the swarms hate us so much," Dot groaned. "What did we ever do to them?"

"It's an ongoing feud dating back, like, a *hundred* years," Simon told her. "That's why wasps get a lot of bad press. Don't you remember learning about it at school?"

"Not really," Dash mumbled.

"That's because you're always on your webbook playing games," Dot said.

"Actually, I've been improving our Binary code!" he protested.

"Your parents could tell you," Simon said. "The swarms started attacking other insects; they wanted to take over the world or something. It wasn't too long ago that they attacked the airport and a bunch of flight attendants working for Ladybird Airlines was stung. They almost killed an innocent microbe who was trying to repair some broken silk, too. I can't *believe* you don't remember!"

"Why do they hate spiders, then?"

"Because we tried to stop them and now that big fat reporter with all the fur is always telling the insect world how terrible they are. *That* can't help our reputation." Simon snapped two of his right legs, trying to recall his name. "Uhm, Terrence Antula, that's it! Before he worked for the Terrantual Times, Terry wrote for the Spider Twines and said all wasps are menaces. As I said, it's an ongoing feud."

"Then they should hate that stupid reporter rather than blaming all of us because of his waspism," Dot said. "This feud has been going on long enough. There's plenty of room for everyone in the insect world!"

"That's grown-ups for you," Simon agreed.

Dash nodded a gesture of hello at the next firefly and shielded his eyes beneath the sudden spotlight. "Which one is Ladybird Airlines again?"

"The ones who wear red and black polka dots," said his sister, rolling her eyes. "Don't you remember the advert with their mascot Lacy Ladybird? Probably not! Here *we* are talking politics and all you can think about is ladybirds in pretty dresses!"

The boys nudged one another playfully as they approached the next street light, which sat on the final corner before they reached the Old Barn. Across the street was O'Tool's, owned by a beetle named Hercules O'Tool and managed by an Irish grasshopper named Diana O'Rear, or 'Big Di O'Rear' to the locals. Simon liked visiting the shop with his mum because of her funny accent. The shop was closed at the moment, though, and the shutters were down.

"Buzz, how's it going up there?" Simon called up to the next firefly.

The light above them flickered on and off a few times to the sound of straining before Buzz's deep, throaty voice cursed and echoed into the night. No matter how hard he squeezed to turn on his butt, he just couldn't hold the beam.

"Ugh, I'm not well," he moaned. "Look out down there—if I squeeze too hard, I might POOP!"

Suddenly, Buzz farted so hard he launched into the air with a WHOOOSHH! leaving a gassy trail behind him like a rocket.

"Catchhh yooouuu laterrrr!"

The children waved as he disappeared through the clouds.

"I wish *I* had a faulty butt!" Dash said.

Left beneath the lamp post in the dark, the three spiders giggled and scurried home.

Chapter Two

Mrs Ranchilla had already ordered supper when Simon and his friends arrived home. They were pleased for the gush of warmth and comfort as she opened the door with a welcoming smile. The twins took off their matching jumpers and wiped their boots, then untied the laces of all twelve between them before following Simon upstairs to his bedroom.

"Supper in thirty minutes!" his mum called after them, organising the boots in neat rows. "I've ordered you all a Mega Muck from McFly's!"

McFly's was a local takeaway, which before the Great Feud sold real maggots and flies as a speciality. Lots of insects, including Simon and his family, publicly protested—times were changing and insects had enough to worry about with WASP attacking at every opportunity; they didn't need to fear being eaten by other bugs, too!

There were plenty of yummy alternatives to enjoy instead, so the company introduced the Mega Muck, a hand-scooped dollop of fresh carrot spew, straight from the mines up north in Spewcastle. McFly's would never go out of business because their supply (particularly when they mined at the weekend) was never-ending. They collected it from what the humans called 'pavements'.

But after their Snail Mail conversation earlier, the kids knew it would be at least an hour before McFly's delivered their supper, leaving plenty of time for Dash to show Simon the new features of Scuttle Bugg, and to work on the twins' Binary code some more.

Simon dumped his bag on the bed, crinkling his cricket cricket sheets which were printed with his favourite cricket players, all of whom were crickets. For a twelve-year-old spider, Simon's room was unusually decorated, as his taste in music and sport was broad. Above his bed was a giant poster of the Beetles, and on the wall beside the window was a horizontal fold-out of a pop group called the Bee Onesies. The lead singer was his biggest celebrity crush. Her name was Honey Bee. In the photo, she was posing in her black and yellow onesie. Beside her was Cherry Bee, dressed in her pink, fruit-printed onesie. At the end stood the only male in the group, Worker Bee, who was often dressed in his construction worker onesie or something similar. In their music videos, his stinger would buzz and shock him as the girls bumbled past.

Simon's mum hadn't approved of the poster at first, but besides a chart detailing the periodic table and a map of the solar system, it was the only indication that Simon was a normal boy. When she had the house to herself, Mrs Ranchilla would also strut around in her own Cherry Bee onesie, singing into her hairbrush. So far, she hadn't been caught!

Dash unzipped Simon's webbook and plopped it on the desk, eager to reconnect to Simon's home Web so they could get started.

Simon caught him just in time.

"Oh, *I'll* do that," he said.

Dash shuffled aside and exchanged a worried glance with his sister.

Dot said, "You're avoiding your emails again, aren't you? It's OK, Bluetooth, I think—"

"No, it's just the connection is a bit fiddly," he said, laughing off her accusation. For a few minutes, he feigned to find a better connection, then closed the lid and shrugged. "Guess it's not working tonight."

Dash raised his brow. "It worked yesterday. Are you *sure* this isn't about what happened in class today?"

"You can tell us," Dot added.

Simon sighed and, convinced this eco-mail would be the worst one yet, he gestured for Dash to give it a shot himself.

When the webbook finally booted up, he admitted, "They send mean messages and call me names."

Dot placed a hand on his shoulder and smiled. "Bluetooth, they're jealous because you're smarter than they are."

"It's not hard to be smarter than Diddit and Ranoff," Dash grumbled, and Dot giggled.

Simon knew he shouldn't take notice of their ridicule. Sure, he hadn't grown into his fang yet but he liked that it was blue—his favourite colour. So what if his voice was still a little squeaky for his age and his legs were skinny? At least he'd passed all nine of their history tests so far with great scores, had two funny friends and a supportive, loving mother. If he spent as much time watching beetleball on television or playing video games as Diddit and

Ranoff did, his grades would probably suck as well.

Simon had never understood the fascination with kicking a maggot around a field to accrue meaningless points, and he much preferred cricket cricket. Honestly, he thought beetleball was a bit violent; a helmet was hardly enough protection for such a small insect playing such a brutal sport, but that maggot was always hyped on adrenaline and yelling at the other team. So much that Simon found it a bit scary. He'd never played beetleball, though; his mum always excused him from class on those days (or at least the letters he forged made it appear that way). Being laughed at fully clothed was torture enough, and Simon wasn't sure he could handle the locker room, too.

"We're in," Dash said, closing Simon's eco-mails.

Out of sight, out of mind, he thought.

Instead, he loaded his mum's disc and a light blue page appeared with a happy-looking bug in the corner.

"This is Scuttle Bugg. You set up a page and upload a photo of yourself, then write messages and updates and post them on the forum. You can find people you know and add new friends."

"Even celebrities?"

"If they have an account," said Dash, glancing at the Bee Onesies poster and grinning. "Other people can share what you write using tags to collate popular topics."

"*Cooool*," Simon said. "When will it go live?"

"Dad says it could be ready by the end of next month," Dot added. "You'll test it for us, won't you Bluetooth?"

Simon nodded. "Sure, count me in." He sighed and tapped the eco-mail icon at the bottom of the screen. "Let's get this over with."

Dot shook her head as she silently started to read the unpleasant jokes Diddit and Ranoff had sent her best friend. She was about to suggest they show his mum when Dash clicked delete and minimised the screen.

"Dungheads," he grumbled. "Ignore them; they'll get bored and pick on someone else."

"I don't think so. *Look* at me, I'm an ideal target."

Dot gestured for Simon to sit down. "Don't say that, Bluetooth, it'll be alright. Perhaps we should tell your mum?"

"No, I don't want to disappoint her." Simon sniffled, wiping his running nose along his hairiest leg. "I already told her I got a date for the prom."

"And *do* you?" she asked.

"No. Diddit and Ranoff are the athletic and funny ones; girls in our class never give me a second glance. It's like I'm invisible!"

"The Winter Prom isn't for another week," Dash said, "and it's lame anyway. Just an excuse for all the popular kids to dress up in pretty frocks and talk about how popular they are with other popular kids."

"*I'll* go to the prom with you," Dot said, taking them both by surprise.

"Eww, gross!" Dash grumbled.

"Shut it, Dungforbrains!" she said. "*You're* just jealous because you'll be going on your own. What do you say, Bluetooth? At least then you're not lying to your mum."

Simon blushed and cleared his throat. "Uh, sure. Maybe we can all go together, though, so we don't leave Dash out."

"Oh, OK, sure," said Dot.

"Maybe we shouldn't have deleted that eco-mail," Simon said, quickly changing the subject.

"I'll get it back," Dash said, fumbling to reconnect to the home Web again with no luck.

"OW!" Bluetooth slapped two legs against his mouth and groaned. "Oh, not again!"

"Are you OK?" Dot pulled his legs away and gasped. "Your fang is glowing!"

"It *hurts*," he said, feeling a pulse of pain as the fang began to vibrate.

Dash waved them over to the webbook. "Uh, guys, look!"

"What is it?" Simon groaned, running his tongue across his achy gums.

"Well, the good news is I got the eco-mail back so we can show your mum," he said, then his eyes widened. "Weird news is I did it without connecting to your home Web."

"That's impossib—OW!" Bluetooth cradled his face again and started to cry, and as he did so the eco-mail disappeared. "I think I need to go to the dentist."

"Do that again," Dash said, pulling Simon's leg away.

The eco-mail re-appeared. Dash moved Simon's leg up and down repeatedly, watching the eco-mail open and close, open and close, open and—

"WILL YOU STOP IT!"

Simon slapped his friend with all his spindly legs, prompting Dash to retaliate until Dot had to intervene and hold them apart with two of her own.

"Stop it, both of you!"

The three spiders stood abruptly at the sound of Mrs Ranchilla's voice calling them for supper.

"This isn't over," Dot said, launching herself into the hall. "Last one downstairs is a slug!"

Chapter Three

The next morning at breakfast, Simon told his mum about his fang ache and how it had been worse before supper, somehow connecting to his webbook.

"Very funny, kids," she said, raising her eyebrows and gesturing for Simon to eat up.

"No Mum, really, and it's been hurting for weeks!"

Dash nodded. "Yeah, last night we were trying to recover this deleted eco-mail that some bullies sent Simon, and his fang glowed and started to vibrate and—"

"Bullies? What bullies?"

"Diddit and Ranoff, two boys in our class," Dot explained. "They've been making fun of his blue fang, but then we realised—"

"Is this true, Simon?"

Simon blushed and glared at the Binary Twins for spilling his secret.

"Yes, but you don't have to—"

"Then we should arrange a meeting with the Head and the boys' parents," she said, slamming down her cutlery, "and I'll call the dentist and make an appointment for later today, alright?"

"Sure, Mum, but don't you think it's weird how my fang vibrated when the eco-mail—"

"Just a coincidence, Dear, I'm sure. If it's not connecting properly, you could ask Mr Spinn nicely if he'll fix your webbook when you see him next."

Simon sighed and wiped his mouth on a napkin. "Sure, Mum. We should go now."

"Hurry along then, kids. And Simon, tell Mrs Longlegs I'll be picking you up before lunch for your check-up."

The three spiders tied their laces and wrapped up warm for a long walk to school. When the door had closed, Simon exhaled a sigh of relief and clapped Dash around the back of his fuzzy head.

"Thanks for that, Dungbum! Now she's going to set up a meeting with Diddit and Ranoff's mum and dad. Paint a target on my back *now* why don't you? I've never been so embarrassed in my entire life!"

"Sorry, mate, I just did what I thought was right."

"She'd have found out eventually, Simon," Dot said. "Better now than when you come home with a broken nose or something."

Simon grunted. "You're right, I know you're right. Sorry, Dash."

Dash slapped him on the back and winked, keeping his voice low so his sister couldn't hear them.

"I'll make it up to you, Bluetooth. Sit next to me in history class, you can copy my answers."

"That's OK, Dash. I studied."

"Oh, then can I still sit next to you?"

Simon smiled. "Alright, but just this once. I don't want to get into trouble; I'm in enough already. Promise you'll start revising?"

Dash crossed his heart with two different legs, then the trio headed to school.

They didn't get far before their path was cut short by Simon's next-door neighbour, an elderly flea named Mr Pond, who was riding his snail bug-gy to the corner shop.

Fleadrick Pond was a slender, pale flea with thinning grey hair and a scrunched-up, grumpy expression. Despite Simon helping with his wheelie bins each week—pulling them up and down his garden path to save his frail legs the trouble—Fleadrick still didn't appear to know his name, nor did he seem interested in learning it.

Simon stopped abruptly so he didn't run into the back of Fleadrick's snail or slip in the thick, bogey-green trail it left on the pavement. Dot and Dash had to swerve around them both to avoid a pile-up.

"Good morning, Mr Pond," Simon said. "Are you going for your newspaper?"

Fleadrick removed the oxygen mask from his face and scowled. "Nothing good about this morning, boy, and it's none of your business. Now, move out of the way or I'll run you over."

"Sorry, Mr Pond," Simon said and rolled his eyes. "I'll come by later for your wheelie bin, OK?"

Fleadrick made a sound a lot like HMPHH! as he replaced his mask.

It was a few minutes before Simon could safely pass the snail, and until then he was stuck staring at its slimy butt and the back of Fleadrick's balding head. As usual, the snail's on-board basket was fastened to the side of its shell and crammed with a folding walking stick, a small oxygen tank and a crinkled shopping bag. Whenever another unsuspecting insect passed by, Fleadrick would tug the snail's antenna to turn at the last minute, using the basket to knock strangers into the street. Then he'd chuckle and continue on his way, beaming with satisfaction.

"Bye, Mr Pond," said Simon, skipping past him to re-join his friends.

When they were a safe distance away, Dash asked, "Who *was* that guy?"

"Oh, that's Fleadrick Pond. He's my neighbour."

"Never seen *him* before."

Simon shrugged. "He keeps to himself, mostly."

"*Mostly?*"

"Yeah, well I help with his bins every week and Mum sometimes mows his lawn."

"Are they friends?" Dot asked.

"No, not really. We don't know much about him, but he does bake nice mud pies. He gave my mum some for Christmas." Simon glanced over his shoulder at the wrinkled old flea and smiled. "Sometimes when I see him in the garden, I like to imagine he has a secret life like he's a ninja or a black belt or something. It makes it easier to ignore his insults."

"Well, he's got the personality for it," Dash said, sniggering. "Come on or we'll be late."

Simon reached up on his tiptoes to push the button on the crossing and waved at the local lollipop man, an overweight centipede named Big Pete. Big Pete wore a yellow hi-vis jacket around his torso and a pair of grey slacks (from which his one hundred legs poked out of and wriggled happily—each one dressed in fluffy socks and ugly brown sandals despite the cold). One side gripped the sign, while the other waved at the now gathering children. His shiny bald head was uncovered and he wore an awkward pair of glasses like headphones, magnifying his failing eyes. They hooked over his head, then bent awkwardly around his face.

"Good morning!" Peter chirped as he entered the street without warning, causing chaos and panic as a variety of huge, fast-moving insects ground to a skidding halt.

"Hey, Peter," said Simon as he passed, high-fiving as many legs as he could.

A few of the waiting insects started to yell HONK! HONK!

"Think that's a new high-five record!" he said.

"Me too, catch you on Monday," Simon said, then hopped up on the pavement.

Simon's usual route to school passed lots of small local businesses and he waved or smiled at their staff along the way. They stopped to exchange pleasantries with the manager of

Shell Shocked, a hip clothing store where Simon and his friends liked to shop for shoes and backpacks with their parents for school. Most of the designs were graffiti or neon-coloured and looked cool because they glowed in the dark.

The owner of the sweet shop Fangtastic wasn't there today, but they stopped to look in the window anyway. Fangtastic sold tangy treats in all different shapes, and Dot and Dash were always challenging one another to see who could eat the most squirmy wormies before their faces turned inside out.

They were most excited to see how well Hercules O'Tool was doing, though; his team of beetles had been working relentlessly to build their new supermarket before the end of the month. Hercules was easy to spot at the back of the site because of his big yellow body and his giant pincer, which he used to carry and move the building materials, much to the young spiders' awe and amazement.

Though he looked terrifying and brutal, Hercules was always jolly and happy to chat about their progress (but today he was deep in conversation, mumbling as he grasped a large metal girder in his mouth, and so hadn't noticed the spiders were there).

Finally, Simon's walk also took him past the Prolice station, a huge building with a wide archway where, he had no doubt, Diddit and Ranoff would end up one day. Everything seemed quiet and uneventful so the spiders paid it no mind, but there were uniformed proactive lice on patrol, as usual, crawling two-by-two and reassuring the locals. Their tall helmets were almost as long as their bodies and caused some of the smaller officers to sway as they marched in formation. They wore white shirts which were buttoned right up to the neck, decorated with a smart blue tie and were *always* tucked in at the waist.

Simon thought he'd make a good Pest Control Station Officer (PCSO) when he grew up because he was great at problem-solving and had lots of friendly acquaintances in the community. If he wasn't so clumsy, one day he might even climb the ranks to join the Cockroach Infestigation Department (CID), or become an Insector to deal with the bullies himself.

But today was not that day.

As the trio rounded the corner near the school, waiting for them at the entrance was Diddit and Ranoff, backed by some other insects Simon didn't know.

"Brace yourselves," said Dash as they approached the front of the building.

Diddit yanked Simon's bag, causing the zip to break and the contents to spill across the pavement. Three spiders stomped on his artwork and ripped the pages of his textbooks, but they seemed to leave him alone after that. Poor Dash, however, wasn't so lucky. Ranoff got him in an uncomfortable headlock and emptied the spider's pockets, stealing his lunch money and the disc containing his mum's BETA version of Scuttle Bugg from his jacket, then tugging his scarf so it tightened around his neck.

"Leave him alone!" Dot cried, attracting the attention of a teacher on the school's stone steps. "Give that back!"

The gang quickly dispersed, scarpering in every direction. Dash unwound his scarf and gasped, then patted his pockets.

"Those Boogerbrains took my mum's disc!"

"It wasn't your fault, Dash," said Simon, gathering his belongings and stuffing them back in his bag. "I'm sure she'll understand."

"Is everything OK?" the teacher shouted.

Dash turned and waved at the teacher. "Fine, Mrs Stinger."

"Hurry up then, the buzzer sounded five minutes ago," she said as they jogged through the door. "You're late!"

Chapter Four

Mrs Longlegs excused Simon for his appointment before lunch, and his mum picked him up at the front of the school. After their encounter with Diddit and Ranoff in the morning, Simon's fang had been aching most of the day.

Brushem and Fillit was Simon's local dental surgery and was owned by two mosquitos. They had both done check-ups for his family in the past, but Simon preferred to speak to Dr Brushem; his brown quiff and pierced wings made him look like a rock star, and although his partner, Dr Fillit was never seen without his white dentist's coat and spectacles, Dr Brushem would fulfil his appointments in a black leather jacket and boots instead, and would stand at the reception desk with his lower legs hung casually on his hips. He also rode an awesome custom snail, with a red and yellow flame-painted shell. It was surprisingly fast for a snail; Simon and his friends were always stunned when Dr Brushem zoomed by.

"What seems to be the problem, Simon?" he asked.

Simon gulped as Dr Brushem sharpened his needle-like nose, ready to inject him with anaesthetic. His assistant, a beautiful, slender dragonfly wearing a white coat and a face mask, was a pleasant distraction.

"My blue fang is aching, and it gets worse when I'm stressed," he explained.

"Open wide!"

Dr Brushem jabbed Simon's gums with his nose, then inspected inside his mouth, poking and prodding his way along his line of baby teeth. Simon tried not to chuckle when a firefly had to come and squat above him, wiggling his butt to give Dr Brushem a bit more light.

"Does this hurt?"

"No," mumbled Simon, spitting a little.

He closed his eyes so he didn't have to stare directly at the firefly's light.

"*Uh-huh*. How about this?"

Simon shook his head this time. The light went out; it was safe to open his eyes again.

"I can't find anything wrong, but if the unusual colour bothers you, we can cap it easily. It's removable, too. We've done it twice before."

Simon's eyes widened. "You mean, there are other spiders around here with blue fangs?"

"*Uh-huh*. Two girls, actually," Dr Brushem said. "You're the first boy I've seen with this condition, though. While we can't change the colour we can certainly hide it with a black covering."

"What do you think, Simon?" asked his mum. "Shall we get it capped?"

"Uh, OK, sure," he said, confident it would give the bullies less ammunition. "Do you think I can get it red and yellow, like your custom snail? That would be *so* cool!"

"From one bright colour to another?" Dr Brushem smirked and smoothed back his quiff. "Sorry, Kid, *ScHnELL* do custom snails, not fangs. You like my snail, huh?"

"It's *amazing!* I love how the shell is really long and shiny, and how you sort of sit back on it and chill out like you're in an armchair."

Mrs Ranchilla reached over and closed her son's jaw, laughing. "Let's not get over-excited."

"Sorry, Mum," he said, blushing. "So will the cap stop me connecting to the Web?"

Dr Brushem raised an eyebrow and turned to Simon's mother. "I'm confused."

She waved it off. "Just a silly joke between Simon and his friends."

"No, it isn't, Mum! It really *did* connect to my webbook—ask my friends! It started to vibrate and glow, and an eco-mail came through. I *swear!*"

"Simon, If you'll excuse us for a moment, I'll have a chat with your mum and we'll be right back." He winked.

Simon exhaled with relief when they all left the room, but he was anxious to know if the cap would block his connectivity. It was a weird superpower to have; he hoped Dr Brushem could fix him. He jiggled his anxious legs in the chair for a bit, explored the blindingly white room, and played with some of the metal instruments. They reminded him of ancient, scary torture devices, and when the door swung open again, Simon almost farted with fright!

"Thank you, Dr Brushem, I'll certainly give them a call," his mum was saying. "It's very kind of you to refer us."

"Of course," he replied. "Let's get you put to sleep Simon and we'll fit that cap."

Dr Brushem grabbed a gas mask from one of the cupboards, suggesting Mrs Ranchilla should to do the same. His assistant entered a few seconds later holding a large glass jar, and sitting in the centre was a brown speckled stink bug named Rodger. She handed the jar to the dentist, prompting Rodger to begin a quick workout routine of star jumps and push ups.

"On my count," said Dr Brushem.

Simon gulped. "Wait, I'm not sure—"

"RELEASE THE BUG!"

Rodger leapt out and Simon was instantly stunned by his DISGUSTING SMELL! He fought the urge to be sick as Roger ran a few laps around the room, filling it with an awful stench. It wasn't long before Simon was unconscious.

Dr Brushem snapped on several pairs of rubber gloves, pulled down a large eye mask that made him look like a scuba diver, then set to work.

***

Simon's mum dropped him off at school just in time for his history quiz with Mrs Longlegs. He'd studied hard and didn't want to miss it. Though he didn't have all his lunch money left (no thanks to Diddit and Ranoff) he was also looking forward to a snack.

Sitting at his usual desk beside Dash, Simon kept his head down and his mouth closed. Already he felt his confidence levels rising and his self-image improving. In the boys' bathroom, he'd seen his new smile in the mirror for the first time.

At the back of the class, Diddit and Ranoff were watching him carefully, probably sensing there was something different about their usual victim.

Mrs Longlegs handed out the quiz papers and told the class to complete them alone and in silence. It would test how much they had been listening to her lectures on the Great Feud, the history of the World Wide Web and the government's roll in protecting its citizens.

Simon read the first question: '*MicrobeSift microbes insert what in order to repair the World Wide Web?*' Simon knew the answer to this one because only yesterday were his friends talking about a WASP attack at the airport.

Enthusiastic and confident he could get another mark, he wrote: '*MicrobeSift microbe workers insert hashtag patches made by spiders into the Web when there has been a slashed or broken connection. Hashtags can also be used as crossroads, depending on the number of horizontal silk threads used.*' Though he didn't include this on the paper, Mrs Spinn had once told him that two horizontal, plus two vertical lines (#) would act as a patch; any more would create a crossroad.

One of his last questions was: '*In relation to the World Wide Web, what does this symbol mean?*' The symbol was @, which Simon had seen many times before. To anyone who knew anything about technology, the answer was obvious. He wrote: *The @ symbol indicates the very centre of the Web,* he wrote, *a server where the most important information is stored and protected by the government at Westspinster*. Though they didn't talk about it in the news often, WASP had been searching for this place since the beginning of the Great Feud, so far with no luck. Even spiders like Mrs Spinn were kept in the dark regarding its location.

Simon slammed his pencil down and sat back in his seat, stretching all eight of his legs one-by-one. He glanced over to see Dash smiling, too. He was slower to finish than Simon but got there eventually. Perhaps this new black-coloured fang would bring them all some better luck, he thought.

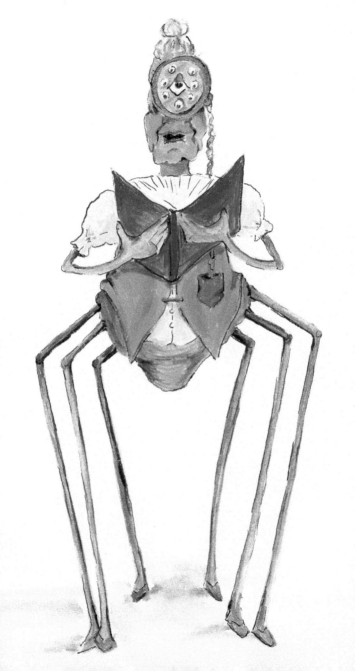

Chapter Five

Mrs Longlegs asked everyone to log in to their webbooks before lunch to be sure they had been eco-mailed their homework for the holidays.

Almost immediately, all the insects in class started to complain.

"Mine won't connect!" complained a young spider at the back.

"Neither will ours," said Ranoff, speaking for both bullies.

Simon noticed Dash tapping to connect on his left, but nothing seemed to be happening. He opened his own and attached the silk as normal, hoping if the system was completely down they wouldn't have to do *any* homework!

"Mine isn't working, either," he told Dash.

Dash scrunched up his nose, then as if being struck by inspiration, he nudged his friend and gestured at his fang. If Simon removed the cap they could finally test their theory.

Simon lowered his head and gently tugged the cap, exposing the glowing blue fang beneath it. He hissed and cupped his face with two legs as it started to vibrate, giving him an instant headache. But Dash was right. The webbook connected!

Simon's face brightened as he kicked his friend sideways across the walkway to get his attention, then pointed at his screen.

It's working, he mouthed, suddenly prouder than he'd ever been of his weird fang.

"Awesome", Dash whispered back, giving him an enthusiastic thumbs up.

Simon sneakily re-covered his fang and watched the access to his eco-mails disappear. Until the connection returned for everyone, as far as Simon and the twins were concerned, there would be no holiday homework.

"Mrs Longlegs, ours aren't connecting either," Simon lied.

"I'll report it, but if the system is still down after lunch, you may all go home," she said, then excused the students for dinner.

The canteen was packed with excited, hungry insects, and they were ordering a variety of meals from knock-off Big Mucks to scoops of carrot spew. Simon wished he could join them in a hearty, gooey meal, but instead he settled for a snack from the vending machine.

There were whispers and complaints circulating about the lack of connection to the World Wide Web and rumours that WASP had attacked several of the silk threads in and out of town, taking down most of the community's access. Simon's palms began to sweat and he wiped them on his jacket; the hair on his legs was slicked to his skin and he must have been pulling a funny face because Dot was the first to ask him what was wrong.

"Nothing," he said, forcing an awkward smile and flashing his new, capped fang.

"That looks good," she said. "Did it hurt?"

"No, he put me to sleep. It ached at first but now it's fine. And it comes off. Look!" he said, removing it just enough to show the blue underneath without causing connection chaos. "Dr Brushem said there are other spiders nearby that have caps, so I'm not alone."

"That's great! Did he say who they were?"

"He gave my mum some information, but wouldn't give their names. They're girls, though."

"I wish *I* had a blue tooth, Bluetooth," Dot giggled. "I know you get bullied, but Dash and

I really like it blue; it's different and fun. Makes you stand out," she said.

"Exactly, which is why I get bullied," he replied.

Dot leaned across the lunch table, resting her head on four fuzzy legs. She smiled. "Well I think it's awesome, and you should wear it blue to prom when we go together."

Simon was about to protest when a huge scoop of yellow-brown spew came soaring across the room and splattered the side of his face. Stunned to silence, Dot and Dash stared at one another then burst out laughing. Most of the canteen followed suit.

"FOOD FIGHT!" Diddit yelled from two tables away.

Simon ducked as another splodge flew their way. He was about to skulk beneath the table, suggesting Dot and Dash hide with him when one of the grasshoppers' friends launched another, larger bowl of spew at the back of Simon's head.

Other children were flinging a variety of nasty-smelling insect food at one another, so Simon dug his hand into a pie beside him, climbed up on top of the table and took aim.

"SIMON, DON'T!" Dash bellowed.

Frustrated and fed up with being their target, Simon loosened his throwing arm and the contents sprayed across the bullies. A spew pie grenade exploded! It showered not only Diddit and Ranoff but their entire group (and even a few teachers!).

Simon jumped down and made a run for it, followed by the Binary Twins.

"Don't look back!" Dot called out.

Simon immediately glanced over his shoulder. The bullies were gaining on them, dripping with spew.

He barged through the doors to the school's grounds. Through his history class and their lunch hour, the temperature outside had dropped and it had started to snow. Simon careened into a tree and threw himself down behind it, hurriedly waving his friends over to take cover.

"We'll never escape if this snow gets any deeper," said Dot. Without her scarf, the hairs on her neck were on end. "What did you go and do *that* for?"

The bullies ploughed through the door after them, then skidded to a halt to search the grounds. Simon and the twins froze, holding their breath.

Dash whispered, "I told you not to throw that pie."

"Yeah, well, they deserved it," Simon mumbled.

Dot groaned, "Ugh, and *we're* going to get detention because *you* hit the teachers!"

"THERE THEY ARE! GET THEM!"

Simon rolled his eyes at Dot's big mouth and set off running across the snow, leaving hundreds of tiny pinprick footprints behind him. The twins caught up, but all three were soon slowed almost to a complete stop as they neared Big Pete's crossing. Spiders were useless in anything more than a flurry. The bullies were lucky; grasshoppers had wings and plenty of energy to lift them high above the piling snow.

Simon, Dot and Dash ducked behind a wall. Pete waved at them and Simon begged him not to give their position away, pointing at the incoming swarm of grasshoppers.

"Everything alright, boys?" Pete asked the grasshoppers.

They landed on the pavement beside him with their hands on their hips and their wings twitching with fury.

Without realising these boys were bullies, Pete wafted the air with all one hundred of his legs and cried, "Phew, you guys smell RANCID!"

"*What* did you say?" Diddit growled. "We smell because we were pelted with spew. We're looking for the losers responsible. Have you seen any spiders?"

Peter swallowed hard, then shook his head. "Not me, but an old flea on a snail slithered by about twenty minutes ago. He went that way." Pete pointed to the school. "No spiders, though."

Diddit's eyes narrowed as he examined Peter's obvious lie. The other grasshoppers were getting bored and some of them were wiping away the spew on their clothes with snow. One was making a snow angel to clean his wings.

"Thanks for nothing," Diddit grumbled.

He shoved Ranoff and his other friends back the way they came. Before they took flight, Diddit cupped a handful of snow and squashed it into a tight snowball, then threw it at Peter's sign and laughed.

"Aren't you a bit fat to be a lollipop bug?" he shouted.

Peter frowned and, using at least fifty of his wiggling legs, scooped up a whole pile of ammunition in just a few seconds.

"Aren't you a bit stupid to say something so mean when you're outnumbered!"

Diddit scowled. "No we're not, *you* are!"

Pete set about the grasshoppers. Not only had they bullied Bluetooth—a friendly, hard-working kid who always said hello to him on a morning—but now they had disrespected his job; a job he loved because it kept the locals—particularly children—safe.

Simon and the twins burst out laughing. They bounded out from behind the wall to help Peter waste his ammunition. With all his hands firing snowballs at once, the grasshoppers were massively outnumbered and overwhelmed. They started to scream and yell at one another, tripping over each other's legs before flying away.

When they were black specs in the distance, Simon and his friends high-fived Pete and cheered and squealed with delight. For once they had beaten the bullies! Simon was sure it wouldn't be the last they'd hear of it, though.

When his shift was over, Peter walked the spiders safely home, shovelling a path through the snow for them with the flat of his sign. He waved them goodbye, then zipped up his yellow jacket and disappeared around the corner.

Simon's mother was shocked to see them home so early. "What's going on, kids?"

"Class Web is down," Dot said, taking off her boots. "We couldn't connect to our webbooks so they said we could go home after lunch if it didn't improve."

"Oh dear," said Mrs Ranchilla, "the home Web is struggling to connect too. I wonder if it's something to do with the weather?"

Dash shook his head. "Oh, no, it's WASP."

She gasped. "What do you mean? There's nothing on the news. Come on in and get warm, we can talk about it over a cup of steamy nectar." She took their jackets and boots and led them into the kitchen where they sat cosily in a circle. "You're covered in snow," she said, "and Dot, it's in your hair!"

"We got into a snowball fight on the way home," Dash explained. "And we won!"

"Let's hope you don't all catch a cold!" She took a sip of her drink and gripped the cup with as many legs as she could fit around it. "What's all this about WASP, then?"

Dash stirred his nectar; he'd never been a fan of this sweet stuff the bee community were raving about, but it smelled good and warmed his frostbitten legs.

"There have been some swarms in the area. The fireflies on the lampposts said there's a temporary blackout," he explained. "We overheard the teachers talking at school."

"I don't think it's because of the weather, Mum," said Simon.

He glanced at his friends and sighed, but they nodded their approval. Now was the perfect time to tell her about his mysterious connecting fang, even if she still thought it was a big joke. If he could demonstrate the skill, they could prove his uncapped fang really *could* connect to the Web without attaching a silk thread. He'd be able to show her the eco-mails he'd been receiving from Diddit and Ranoff (though it would mean he'd have to do his holiday homework).

"Mum, about my fang—" he said.

She hummed and leaned forward. "Are you happy with it?"

"It's great," he said, smiling, "but you know I said before how it connects to the Web?"

She rolled her eyes and sighed, then slapped the table and took her cup to the sink.

"I told you before, Simon, that's impossible and it's not very funny—"

"What if we could show you?" Dot said, taking Mrs Ranchilla by surprise.

"I doubt it, Dear."

"Simon, do you have your webbook?"

"I'll get it," Dash said, scuttling off down the hallway to retrieve Simon's school bag. He returned a few seconds later and placed it on the kitchen table, then turned it on. "We can prove it works and get you reconnected."

Intrigued by the depth of their prank, she gestured for them to give it a go. Perhaps when it failed they could drop the joke and move into the living room. She wanted to see if there was anything on the local news channel about WASP attacks and if there were any preventative measures to take.

Dash turned the screen to face Mrs Ranchilla and pointed to the little web symbol in the bottom corner of the screen. It had a red line through it, indicating there was no connection. Once satisfied, Simon removed the cap from his fang and instantly winced with pain as it began to glow and vibrate. After a few seconds of stunned silence, Mrs Ranchilla gasped when the symbol lit up yellow and Simon's inbox popped up on screen.

"*Now* do you believe me?" he said.

"Is this some kind of magic trick?"

"It's my fang, Mum," he insisted, opening his mouth as wide as he could to show her. "We were telling the truth."

"And this is why you've been in so much pain recently?" She cupped his face and chewed her bottom lip with concern. "We'll get you another appointment to see Dr Brushem first thing tomorrow morning."

"Mum, there's nothing he can do." Simon replaced the cap and the connection dropped again, causing Mrs Ranchilla to sit down in shock.

"I can't believe it, and I don't understand how —"

"Mrs Ranchilla," Dot interrupted, "didn't Dr Brushem say there were others in our community who had blue fangs capped too?"

"Yes, but I don't see how—"

"Maybe they have the same ability?"

Dot stood to pour Mrs Ranchilla another cup of nectar; she always found a hot, sweet drink helped when she was upset, so she hoped it would work for Simon's mum, too.

"Do you still have their numbers, Mum?"

She nodded. "I haven't called them yet."

"Can't we call them now?" Simon asked.

Mrs Ranchilla's legs began to judder nervously. Simon reached out and held one of them with his. Bluetooth had been both a nickname and an insult used against him for as long as he could remember; other insects had been cruel in school and in the streets, and although he now had the opportunity to hide it and forget, suddenly he wasn't so keen. WASP was a serious threat to their community. In *his* mouth sat the answer to their problems.

"I haven't always been able to do it, Mum, and maybe soon I won't be able to any more. I don't know how long it will last. We should make the best of it while we can."

"But you were a perfectly normal child," she told him.

"I'm *still* normal," Simon said grumpily.

Mrs Ranchilla beamed and squeezed his shoulder. "Oh, Simon, Sweetheart, of course you are. I only meant—"

"I know, it's OK, Mum. It would be nice to meet others with fangs like me, though; people who are different."

If Simon could connect to the World Wide Web without the need for a thread, then other bugs with blue fangs might be able to, too. That could be the start of a solution, even if only temporarily, because without a physical web to destroy, WASP would be powerless to terrorise them.

"You're not different," Dot told him. "Perhaps you're just special."

"But I don't want to be special," he said, "and if I am, it means my talent is useless and goes to waste. Please, Mum, let's call the number. What harm could it do?"

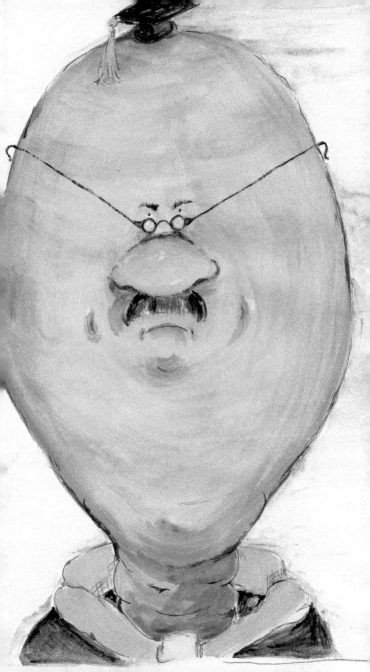

Chapter Six

B est friends Diddit and Ranoff had known each other for as long as they could remember. They went to the flea circus every month when they were little, to grasshopper summer camp three years in a row, and they competed on the same beetleball team in school. So when Diddit suggested to Ranoff that they load up Mrs Spinn's social media disc and give it a try, he couldn't say no; it sounded like fun they might get into deep trouble for later, and *that* was their favourite kind of trouble.

It was too late to be on school grounds, but the pair often crept in when it got dark to hang out with their friends. Today it was just the two of them—the perfect time to connect to the class Web and try out the stolen disc.

"What if the connection is still down?" Ranoff asked.

Diddit shrugged. "Then we'll go home and try it there instead."

To their surprise, the connection appeared to be working again.

A very busy microbe had been repairing WASP slashed silk all afternoon just around the corner. There was no telling how long it would last, though, not with the attacks getting worse and more frequent. The microbe had heard the distant humming of buzzing wings as WASP flew overhead in strict formation, looking for an ideal thread to slash or a weakened spot to infect with virus vibrations. He imagined their narrow eyes hidden behind a pair of thick flight goggles and pictured their bomber jackets flapping in the wind.

Diddit and Ranoff loaded one of their webbooks and connected it to the class Web, then installed the program.

On the screen appeared an amazing platform where insects of all species could connect and chat. Diddit suggested they should both create profiles and show them off to their friends over the weekend.

In a small house across town, a little red flag popped up on someone's screen, followed by a loud BING BONG! alert.

"Can you hear someone?" Ranoff whispered.

The sound of slithering and the gentle glow of the security guard's slimy body drew nearer.

Gary the glowworm took his job very seriously, which was to protect the school from trouble-makers and bug-lers. He was sure he'd heard giggling in the history classroom. Using the luminescence from his body to light the corridors as he patrolled, he wriggled his way to the source of the commotion, then rounded the corner and yelled 'AHA! GOTCHA!'. The classroom was empty.

Gary shrugged and straightened some of the chairs, then continued on his usual route, keeping an eye on the door to the history classroom just in case.

The two grasshoppers sprinted behind the building, using their wings to increase their speed. They rounded the corner and crouched beside the bins to catch their breath. There was a foul stench of rotten food back there, no doubt from the kitchen staff dumping leftovers in the general waste bin. But there was also an overflowing pile of paperwork and books from the recycling bin.

"Look what *I* stole today," Diddit said.

He rummaged in his pocket and pulled out a small silver lighter. He flicked it open. A tiny yellow flame appeared and he bent to set a ripped maths books alight.

"I always hated algebra."

Ranoff grabbed his wrist to stop him. "Dude, you're playing with fire."

It was too late. The book was burning brightly. It was so hot Diddit had to drop the lighter or scold his legs. As it hit the rest of the pages, the entire bin set alight, leaving the grasshoppers staring at it in awe.

"Oh no! Look what you did!" Ranoff cried. "Help me put it out!"

"No way, let's get out of here or we'll get caught by Gary," said Diddit.

Then Diddit and Ranoff ran off.

It only took a minute or two for Gary to see an amber glow through one of the classroom windows, and he wriggled as fast as his chubby, slimy body could carry him out to the alley behind the school. *All* the bins were on fire now! The flames licked the window of the staff room where they would no doubt catch the curtains, then the carpet, then the rest of the building!

Not on my watch!

Gary immediately called the emergency services and used a bottle to squirt some water over the flaming books. He slithered back and forth from the pond to fetch more as he waited. Thankfully, it wasn't long before he could hear sirens coming over the hill.

Bugs of all different colours turned up. They were gigantic beside Gary who, because he was feeling anxious, was now twice his usual brightness, acting as a beacon for them on the horizon. First, he heard the HONK! HONK! of the dark red fire beetles and saw the ominous glow of their crimson and orange antenna. They flashed as they drove down the street. In preparation for the fire, they were already swirling saliva around in their mouths, building up a good amount to spit on the fire in unison at their Captain's call.

Escorting them was the WHEW! WHEW! of the Prolice metallic-blue beetles. Their shells reflected their flashing aqua antenna as they told passers-by to 'move aside, please'. It was their job to keep everyone safe, clear the area and, if necessary, help track down the arsonist. First, though, there would be an infestigation to figure out the cause.

Behind them Gary heard the NEE-NAW! of green medical beetles; these guys moved fast and with purpose. The white cross markings on their back and their flashing green and white antenna indicated they were heading to a life or death situation. Lots of insects on the road pulled aside to let them pass.

Gary pointed to the fire as everyone pulled up in a flurry of chaos and commotion. The red beetles approached the fire. Careful not to dribble or spill any of their salivae, they waited for their Captain to yell the orders to SPIT! SPIT! SPIT! On the count of three, they spat huge globules of saliva onto the fire until it started to go out. There was a loud PSSSSST! as the fire was extinguished. Immediately, they packed up and scuttled out of the way for everyone else to do their jobs. Gary was stunned at their speed; less than twenty seconds at the scene and already the fire was out!

From beneath the Prolice beetles' wings hopped hundreds of smaller officers, all in their smart uniforms and moving in marching formation. They fanned out to create a perimeter and from a distance looked like blue crime scene tape, which established a 'do not pass' zone.

As Gary watched the commotion, one of the medics approached him and lifted his wing to offer a safe, sheltered place to wait. Physically, the glowworm was unharmed but he was a bit shocked and feeling guilty; it was *his* job to prevent such incidents.

"I'm fine," he told the medic. "Was there anyone inside?"

"The Prolice are checking now, Sir," he replied. "Can I take you to the hospital?"

"No, no, I'm not injured. Thank you."

"How about a drink of water?" the beetle persisted. "Can you breathe OK with all this smoke?"

The beetle stepped back and began to beat his wings at a high speed to fan Gary with some cool air. Gary fought for words as a huge gust caught his breath, causing his lips to flap and wobble when he spoke.

"I'm—fine—thank—you!"

"Are you sur—"

"FOR THE LAST TIME I'M—" Gary yelled.

Feeling guiltier, he forced a smile and waited with the medic until the smoke had changed from a thick, dirty brown to a soft grey-white colour.

"Sir, may we ask you a few questions?" asked a small red beetle.

It was this beetle's job to carry the equipment for the fire department, and he got to ride on the back of one of his larger colleagues. He had a stern, solid face and a tiny black moustache.

"If you're feeling up to it," he added.

Gary nodded. "Of course, just shocked."

"Did *you* find the fire?"

"Yes, I was in one of the classrooms and saw it through the window."

"Do you work at the school?"

"I'm the night guard," he confirmed, flashing his name tag proudly. "I raced out to see what was going on and the bins were on fire. I tried to put it out with my water bottle before it got worse, but I was too late."

"When you say *raced*—" the beetle began, gesturing at Gary's slimy body. "How long before you arrived at the scene?"

Ashamed, Gary lowered his head. "Several minutes. I try and try to slither faster, but I'm slippery, you see."

"OK, Sir. You did the right thing calling us. Did you see anyone else around?"

Gary gasped. "Oh, you don't think someone did this on purpose, do you?"

"Well, we found a lighter beside one of the bins. It may have been an accident, but we're currently looking at arson. The Prolice have insisted we call the CID."

"But I didn't see anyone," Gary said. "I'd have caught them, I know I would!"

The beetle held out the lighter for Gary to examine, but he didn't recognise it. Most of the teachers had quit smoking to set a good example for the children.

Gary shook his head. "I can't believe someone just did it and ran off. Why wouldn't they report it? Someone could have been killed!"

"Fear of the consequences, I imagine," said the red beetle. "Do you know if any of the children returned to the school this evening for any reason?"

"No, I would have seen them," he said, straightening up. "*Nobody* gets past me!"

"I see. Thank you for your time, Sir. If you could wait here, the Cockroach Infestation Department will want to speak to you when they arrive."

Gary found an uncomfortable wooden bench to sit on as he watched the emergency services at work, waiting for the CID to arrive. The Prolice must have been really concerned to call for an additional team, perhaps because of the nature of the fire and the seriousness of it being set on school premises. During the daytime, there could have been hundreds injured and they would have had to evacuate the school!

Gary hoped the Head wouldn't fire him.

There were still lingering Prolice and plenty of choking smoke drifting across the grounds when the CID arrived. Thousands of cockroaches swarmed the scene, covering every inch of the school building inside and out with their long brown bodies. Within five seconds, the entire school and its grounds looked to be alive as they thoroughly inspected it. They were EVERYWHERE!

Gary suddenly found himself surrounded by six cockroaches. They all had notebooks (filled almost completely with untidy handwriting and pointless observations).

"Did you see the arsonist?"

"Did you hear any voices?"

"How long did it take you to get to the fire?"

"When did you decide to call the emergency services?"

"Who else was on the premises?"

"Did anything suspicious happen beforehand?"

Gary couldn't take the rapid-fire questions any longer, because he could barely hear and understand one before the next overlapped and overwhelmed him. Two of the questions he did catch stuck in his mind. He told the cockroaches that he had checked the history classroom because he thought he heard laughter. But it was empty, he insisted.

"Gets lonely doing my job, fellas, and it's not unusual for the shadows and echoey halls to play tricks on me," he admitted, "or for kids to sometimes set up pranks—they mean well."

"I don't think they did on this occasion," said one of the cockroaches.

"Me neither."

"Nor me."

"Neither did I," said another.

Most of the cockroaches had finished their swift infestigation by now and were turning to face him; with thousands of pairs of eyes staring at him, Gary felt he was the insect being infestigated! The further back in the crowd a cockroach stood, the louder its voice became.

"I DON'T EITHER."

"I AGREE!" said another.

"ME TOO!"

Gary's glow was beginning to dim from exhaustion. He wanted to go home and slip into bed.

"I can't tell you anything else, fellas," he admitted, then slowly began to slither away when they had nothing further to ask him.

Eerily, they watched until Gary was out of sight, then robotically turned and swarmed another witness, an elderly flea. He had been riding past the school on his snail bug-gy when he saw two lanky grasshoppers fleeing the scene.

***

Fleadrick Pond's evening had been ruined by the CID's persistent questions. Frankly, he deemed their whole department to be overly enthusiastic, always focused on the wrong people and searching the wrong places. He'd seen them scattering across the outside of the building, covering it with their ugly brown bodies as they gathered all the right evidence, but not necessarily in the right order. In Mr Pond's opinion, after interviewing the night guard, the next logical step was to check any security cameras. Every school had them, and as the bins were beside the exit to the kitchen, any students messing around back there would've been immediately captured on the footage.

But Mr Pond already knew the identities of the two grasshoppers. He'd been doing some research of his own recently into the WASP attacks and had stumbled upon a discarded disc in his neighbour's garbage a few days ago. It allowed him access to Scuttle Bugg, Mrs Spinn's new social media platform. The disc was a live version of Scuttle Bugg, though it hadn't yet been made available to the wider public. Fleadrick loved a challenge and spent most of his time playing with technology or spying on his neighbours, documenting their every move and reporting anything suspicious.

They deemed him a miserable old flea with nothing better to do than snoop and ride his snail around town. Fleadrick thought of himself more like the public servant his community couldn't do without.

He loaded Scuttle Bugg when he arrived home and had refuelled his snail, thanking him for the ride. Then he hunched at his desk and scoured the servers for anything related to the incident at the school while the snail ate.

Claire Spinn's test account was the first thing he found, alongside accounts for her twin children Dot and Dash Spinn, who were friends with the spider next door, a nice (if a little unusual) young lad who helped him with his bins each week.

Fleadrick's connection to the home Web flickered a little and he gave his webbook a prompt, harsh smack to bring it back again.

"HMPH," Fleadrick grumbled, "none of these problems back in my day!"

It happened a couple more times as he was typing. Fleadrick gave it another slap. He assumed somewhere in the neighbourhood a microbe was hard at work fixing the silk—he would just have to be patient.

And Fleadrick was right. At the end of his street at the nearest connection box, a busy microbe got an electric shock every time Fleadrick attempted to reconnect!

"Ouch!" he cried, wondering which of the residents was trying to interfere. "STOP IT! THAT HURTS!"

Suddenly (and thankfully, for the microbe's sake), Fleadrick stopped typing. An alarm sounded and a little red flag appeared on his screen. Two new accounts had been created on Scuttle Bugg. With no surprise, they both belonged to the grasshoppers he'd seen in town. Not only were they at the school, but he'd seen them being anti-social before, picking on anyone younger. Earlier, he was sure they'd been throwing snowballs at his neighbour, Simon.

Fleadrick scowled and took a screen capture of each new account. His face brightened when he clicked on Diddit's page, though, because the foolish bully had been taking selfies with the lighter and setting fire to books. In the background, Ranoff could be seen trying to hide his face with his wings.

"Must be linked to the worm they were interviewing," he grumbled, then captured another copy of Diddit's selfie.

Fleadrick quickly attached what he'd found to an eco-mail and sent it to an old friend. He titled his eco-mail 'Intelligence submission for today's fire', then tapped his fingers on the keys, anticipating their reply. It took a few minutes, but as always his contact sent a response to confirm they were looking into it and appreciated the information. At the bottom of the eco-mail, it stated: 'Keep up the good work—you're one of our best agents, Mr Pond'.

Satisfied with his contribution, Fleadrick nodded and decided his reward would be a nice hot cup of nectar. He'd earned it! He'd been out in the snow all day; both he and his snail were tired and chilly. In fact, his snail had already disappeared into his room and dozed off! Fleadrick had done (in less than thirty minutes) what the Cockroach Infestation Department hadn't managed to achieve in a whole evening.

Fleadrick logged off Scuttle Bugg and stowed the disc safely in his desk's pigeonhole.

Claire Spinn would never know he and his friends had access to the content because, other than the young grasshoppers, only Claire and those she'd authorised were given versions of the early release. From Fleadrick's research, it seemed the disc's only purpose was to install a shortcut to your webbook's desktop and it downloaded a few pages of instructions and development notes. If you searched for Scuttle Bugg online, you could read about the upcoming launch, but members of the public were unable to set up accounts or interact with anyone.

Fleadrick Pond had found a nice back passage into Claire Spinn's brand new system —a system which, in a few weeks, would be a hive of intelligence and, no doubt, low-level criminal activity. In other words, it was a gold mine!

Chapter Seven

Mrs Ranchilla dialled the number on the scrap of paper given to her by Dr Brushem. She and the children gathered around it anxiously.

It rang once.

It rang twice.

It rang three times and—

"Hello, Spinn household."

Dot and Dash's mouths fell open in unison, and if not for their clothing, Simon would have thought the twins were a mirror image. Dot swallowed hard. She was the first to speak because even Mrs Ranchilla was stunned to silence.

"*Mum?* Is that you?"

"Dot, why aren't you at school?"

"Mum, can you come over to Simon's house?" she asked. "It's important."

"What's the matter? Are you both OK?"

Mrs Ranchilla snapped out of her trance and cleared her throat, then swiped the phone from

Dot's hand to take over the conversation. Perhaps she should be explaining this to their mother rather than three young children with wild imaginations! She didn't want Claire to panic.

"Claire, it's me. Listen, I'm sorry if we alarmed you. Could you pop round this evening at some point with your husband? Simon's dentist gave me your telephone number and said you might know something about a problem he's been experiencing with his—hmm, yes of course—absolutely, we won't tell anyone else—oh, yes—we'll wait for you right here. Thanks, Claire. Goodbye."

Mrs Ranchilla instructed Simon and the twins to stay in the kitchen and wait for Mrs Spinn to arrive; she had something very important to tell everyone. She placed a large plate of sticky mud pies in the middle of the table and said they shouldn't connect to the World Wide Web or leave the house, either— not until she'd spoken with Mrs Spinn.

With so many pies to get through, they were more than happy to stay put!

When Mrs Ranchilla went upstairs, Simon reached for a pie and (despite having lots of questions and plenty of opinions on what Mrs Spinn had said on the phone), he could only chew in thought. What could Mrs Spinn possibly want to tell them?

"What do you suppose *that* was about?" Dash asked, breaking the silence as if he had read Simon's mind.

Simon tried not to spit pie at him when he replied, "Dunno, but I'm worried."

"Don't be," Dash said. "My mum's cool."

"I know, but you've got to admit this *is* a bit weird!"

Twenty-five minutes later there was a loud knock at the front door and Simon scurried to let Mrs Spinn in out of the snow. He was glad, really, because they were beginning to feel sick after stuffing in all those mud pies! Simon had been unable to beat his previous record of eating six before he'd been sick. Dash was still the champion.

Claire shook the snow off her hairy legs, then untied her shoes and hung up her coat. She shuddered and sniffled, pleased to be warm and dry again.

"Sorry I'm late," she said to Mrs Ranchilla, who was on her way down the stairs. "It's *awful* out there."

"That's alright, Claire. Where's Mr Spinn. Working?"

"Clive's stuck because of the weather. He'll be late home," she said, gesturing at the deepening snow and rolling all of her beady eyes, "but I've spoken to him over the phone. We both agree it's time we discussed this. I'm pleased Dr Brushem finally recommended we talk."

Simon quickly shut the door and turned the key. He followed the adults into the kitchen and sat down beside his friends.

"Can *you* help me with my blue fang, Mrs Spinn?" Simon asked.

Claire shuffled closer to her daughter and squeezed her hand. "Dot, Dear, would you open your mouth for me, please?"

Dot scowled and glanced across the table at Simon whose face was scrunched with concern. Why would Claire need to look inside *her* mouth and not his?

Dash nodded his approval when Dot's eyes met his; their mother would never do or say anything unless it was in their best interest. She was one of the most intelligent spiders in their community, so Dash knew she had a plan. Whatever she was about to do, he was confident it would solve all their problems.

Dot opened her mouth. Her mother reached inside and fumbled with her largest fang for a couple of seconds, mumbling as she did so. There was a loud POP! and Dot's black fang came away in her palm.

She gasped. "Mum! Did you just pull out my fang?"

Her eyes began to well with tears and her bottom lip quivered. She hadn't felt the tooth come loose at any point, and couldn't understand how it had fallen so painlessly from her gum. When the dentist performed her check-ups, she always found them uncomfortable until he put her to sleep.

"It's alright," Claire told her, patting her shoulder. "It's not real."

She reached into her handbag for a mirror and held it up. Dot pulled back her lips and the room gasped.

"I don't understand," said Dot, staring at her reflection. "*I* have a blue fang too? Does everyone?"

Simon's eyes widened with delight. He jumped from his seat. "I'm not the only one! I'm not the only one!"

Claire began to laugh. She reached into her mouth to remove her own cap, revealing another blue tooth. Simon's glowed but theirs sparkled, however, all three vibrated at the same frequency. It varied based on your family tree, he concluded, but Simon hadn't inherited his fang so he was confused.

Dot smacked her hands against her mouth, alarmed by the weird and unfamiliar sensation.

"It's just us so far," she told her daughter. "Your father and I felt it was best to cap both our fangs until we could learn more about their capabilities. As far as we knew, nobody else in our town had them, but then you started school and met Simon. We were delighted but concerned."

"Why didn't you say something to us sooner?" Mrs Ranchilla asked. "If Dot inherited hers from you, why not Dash, and where did Simon get his?"

"We weren't sure Simon's had the same abilities," she explained, "and though I'm confident Dot inherited hers from me, there's really no explanation beyond that right now. Personally, I think it's a natural evolution; a way to bypass the need for silk and protect ourselves from WASP."

Dash was desperate to pull a cap from one of his teeth. "I want one too!"

"I think you take after your father," Claire said, grinning. "Unfortunately, Dot inherited *my* unusual smile. But it's OK, because having a blue tooth can't hurt you, and it doesn't have to be visible. Each time Dot went to the dentist," she told Mrs Ranchilla, "Dr Brushem simply increased the size as she grew. We've been experimenting with mine, but haven't had much luck. We *did* create something else pretty cool, though."

Dot said, "Ah, so *that's* why you always had to put me to sleep!"

Claire nodded. "Everyone has to be put to sleep for a cap the first time because it's painful, but Dr Brushem put *you* to sleep *every* time! We didn't want you to find out."

"And now you've found a way to give everyone *else* blue teeth?" Dash asked, excitedly.

"Possibly. They're not ready yet, but we have some final designs. They're going to be available in different colours and will be a new fashion accessory for all insects; we think kids will love them, especially spiders. You guys could be our models!"

"For what purpose, though?" Mrs Ranchilla asked, pouring everyone some hot spew and opening another box of mud pies.

Claire paused for a moment, causing Simon and the children to glance at one another suspiciously.

After a few seconds, she said, "They'll prevent bullying and take the spotlight off

E. Rachael Hardcastle & David Hardcastle

Simon and Dot for a while. She told me about the eco-mails you've been getting."

Simon blushed. "You did all this for us?"

"And anyone else out there hiding the same secret."

"Oh, wonderful!" Mrs Ranchilla said, squeezing Simon in a tight, unexpected embrace. "You've been so worried about the other kids calling you Bluetooth. Soon you won't have to be. *Everyone* can be a Bluetooth, or a Greentooth, or a Yellowtooth! Maybe I should get a pink one," she mused. "What do you think?"

"Sure, Mum, that would be cool."

"You'd look great," Dot said, still fidgeting and going cross-eyed when she tried to see her tooth without the mirror. "Ours are real though, Simon. I can't believe it!"

"Me neither!"

"You're not mad, Dot?" Claire asked.

Dot shook her head and beamed across the table at Simon, who was grinning from ear to ear.

"I understand why you didn't tell me. I'm not ashamed. It makes us special."

Claire winked at Simon then stood to excuse herself. "My husband will be home soon. I should be getting back."

"Well thanks, Claire," said Mrs Ranchilla. "Don't worry, we won't say a word to anyone about your invention, will we Simon?"

"Of course not," he said.

While Claire was putting her coat on, she agreed to let Dot and Dash sleep over again at Simon's house.

"Maybe you could go and see Dr Brushem for me?" she told the young spiders when Mrs Ranchilla was out of the room. "I'm sure he'd show you all the different colours we have planned. Wouldn't that be fun?"

"Sure," said Simon. He was excited to ask Dr Brushem about his custom snail as well as learn more about the new cap designs. "We'll go tomorrow after breakfast."

Mrs Spinn gave both her children a tight cuddle and a kiss on the head before she disappeared into the street.

The snow was falling lightly now, and through the haze they could see the fireflies on duty lighting her way as she struggled home.

Chapter Eight

After breakfast, Simon and the twins waded through the snow to see Dr Brushem, grateful the skies were now powder blue and clear. Dot and Simon walked ahead of Dash to chat about their fangs, which they'd left uncapped. Simon thought the dentist might like to examine them together and check for similarities. Not only were they the same colour but they could *both* connect to the World Wide Web in the same way, at the same speed, and with the same symptoms.

Simon was beginning to get used to the vibrations. Though he was happy to talk with Dot and Dash on the way there, when anyone passed them in the street they closed their mouths.

Curious about his fang's reach, Simon had been experimenting without the twins most of the morning; he'd been up early thinking about how all this time he'd felt so alone when his best friend and biggest crush at school *also* shared his quirk!

Simon unplugged as much as he could from the home Web when he woke, leaving the twins to sleep. He walked slowly around the Old Barn to test how and when his fang found a connection. Surprisingly, he didn't have to wait long. In mere seconds, Simon's fang began to vibrate as he passed his own webbook on the desk. It did so again when he passed his mother's bedroom and the office, clearly finding other devices and buzzing in response.

Simon scuttled downstairs and sat in front of the television. That connected too, though it took a bit longer.

Overall, his experiment was a success. It seemed most items within his house would connect without the use of a silk thread when he uncapped his fang. When he covered it again, immediately the connections would drop and he'd have to plug everything back in manually again. It was a fascinating hour (but a bit of a strange way to start his day).

He told Dot all about it when she joined him for breakfast, then briefed Dash when he slumped in the chair twenty minutes later, still wearing his pyjamas.

It was obvious Dash was feeling left out by the way he dawdled behind his friends now; occasionally, he'd kick a stone or make a snowball, then launch it as hard as he could at the closest tree or lamppost. As the snow began to melt and turn to slush the further from Simon's house they walked, Dash found a dirty puddle to splash in, giving his sister a reason to yell at him when he wet her jacket.

"I think he's jealous," she whispered to Simon.

"Me too. Maybe we should talk about something else until we get there?"

"Like what? I'm too excited!"

Simon quickly covered his mouth with his scarf when he saw Mr Pond's snail round the corner ahead. The old flea had been to the shop for a newspaper and was heading straight for them, refusing to swerve or wait for anyone else.

Simon tipped his head to his neighbour and, strangely, received a pleasant smile and a '*Morning*, Simon' in return. That would play on Simon's mind for the next ten minutes as he listened to Dot trying to engage Dash in some kind of beetleball conversation.

"Did anyone else just hear Mr Pond say good morning to me?"

Dash shrugged. "So what if he did?"

"I don't think he's *ever* smiled at me, and anything he says is always rude."

Dot hummed. "Perhaps he got some good news, or is pleased the snow's melting? It can't be easy riding a snail in this weather."

"I'll bet he ran over someone," Dash grumbled. "When we get to the crossing there will be a Big Pete shaped angel in the snow. All that will be left of him is that big yellow vest!"

Simon laughed but he was still a bit worried.

Fortunately for Pete, Dash was wrong and Fleadrick hadn't squashed him in the snow. He was working overtime until the snow cleared, ensuring everyone managed to make it safely across the busiest road.

Today he was wearing an extra large pair of boots and his usual vest, but any hands not holding his sign were gloved and stuffed in various pockets. For the three spiders, his presence was a blessing because Simon was anxious about that road. What if he got the hair on his little legs stuck to the ice? What if a big bug drove by before he could free himself, and he wound up as road kill; a smudge on a passing beetle's shell? He shuddered at the thought.

"Where are you lot off to?" Pete asked, waving them across the road.

Simon and the twins high-fived him as usual, but they didn't manage to beat their record. They explained they were on their way to see the dentist.

Pete cringed. "Never did like the dentist," he said, "but that Dr Brushem has an awesome custom snail. Have you seen it?"

"Yes!" Dash exclaimed. "We're hoping to see it again today. It's so cool!"

"You bet it is! I admire it every day on my way home. He got it sprayed by that workshop across town. *ScHnELL* it's called. That's German for 'fast', did you know? They paint all kinds of artwork on like flames and racing stripes or even flowers. I heard some of them red fire beetles weren't actually red, so to join the fire department they had to get a re-spray!" Pete laughed, holding his wobbly belly.

"Maybe they'll be able to spray paint some crutches on my front legs, then I can get out of doing PE forever!" Dash said, laughing.

Simon giggled too. His friend was slowly perking up. It was just like Dash to think of an unrealistic scheme so he could skip a class, particularly one he wasn't very good at. Simon hated seeing him sulk, especially knowing he and Dot were the cause.

"That would never work," Dot said, rolling her eyes.

Dash scowled. "Worth a try."

"Yeah, but is it worth detention?" asked Simon.

He and Dot high-fived as they hopped up on the kerb and the three spiders waved goodbye to Big Pete.

They made it to the dentist safely and without further argument about the crutches, though Simon couldn't help but grin as the creative cogs in Dash's brain continued to turn.

Dr Brushem welcomed the spiders into his office and they sat together in the waiting room. It was a few minutes before opening time, and the mosquito didn't have his first appointment for at least another hour. Therefore, they had plenty of time to talk.

"Did my mum call you about the designs?" Dot asked.

The doctor nodded and fumbled behind the reception desk for some large pieces of paper. He shoved aside an old Slug and Lettuce magazine, then spread his notes out on the table for the children to see. They were intricate!

Simon thought they looked like an architect's blueprint because they were so detailed and thorough.

Claire Spinn and Dr Brushem had planned to start with seven different colours. They were: blue, green, red, pink, purple, yellow and orange. Some of them could be varnished with glitter!

Dot's eyes widened; she fumbled with her blue fang, dreaming about how pretty it might look in pink.

"Like a disco ball," she gasped. The boys glanced at her, confused, so she quickly added, "Sorry, I was just thinking aloud. The glitter ones look like little disco balls."

Simon scrunched up his face with disapproval, but Dash hadn't ruled out the glitter blue, or even the glitter green. He'd been envious of the way Simon's fang glowed naturally when it connected to the World Wide Web, and he wanted to get as close to that as possible.

"Why do *you* want one?" he asked his sister. "You have the real thing!"

Dot blushed. "I like pink."

"If you wear any more pink you'll be camouflaged against your bedroom walls," he murmured.

Dot scowled at him and shook her head.

Dr Brushem laughed at their bickering. "There will be plenty for everyone, and we'd like to encourage people your age to try them first over the holidays. We think they'd make a nice fashion accessory. You'd be trendsetters."

"We'd *definitely* be popular then!" Simon told Dot.

"Surely you don't want to be popular?" Dash argued, folding his arms and slumping back on the dentist's uncomfortable sofa.

"What do you mean?" Dot asked.

"You hate the popular kids because they bully you. They bully *us*! The more attention they get, the nastier they become. Why would you want to be like them?"

"We wouldn't be," Simon assured him. "We could change what it means to be popular. Everyone can be popular with your mum's invention."

"You say that *now*, but it won't be long before you're ignoring me in the halls and throwing food at me in the canteen because *your* fangs are originals."

"We already throw food at you." Simon bumped him shoulder-to-shoulder. "We're best friends, Dash, and we always will be."

Dr Brushem rolled up the design plans and replaced them with a new document. This was much more detailed and stamped across the top in red ink were the words: TOP SECRET. Instantly, this held the young spiders' attention.

"Whoa, what's this?" Dash asked, leaning forward to get a good look.

"This is what your mother and I wanted you to see," Dr Brushem said.

Dot asked, "Not the designs?"

"Partly, but we need your help with something else. What I'm about to show you is very important and you can't tell anyone. You have to promise not to share our secrets."

"Can't I tell my mum?" Simon asked.

The mosquito shook his head frantically, and Dot had to duck to avoid being poked by his long nose!

"Not even your mum."

"Can we tell ours?" Dash asked, wide-eyed.

Dot elbowed him. "They're in on it already, Dungforbrains!"

"Oh, yeah, right!"

"And if you tell anyone, I'll use you as WASP bait," Dr Brushem warned.

Dash sniggered. "WASP bait, HA! HA!"

But Dr Brushem wasn't laughing. He made them put their hands in the centre of the table, one on top of the other, to swear they wouldn't tell anyone about the secret.

"Now we're agreed, I can show you the *real* plans for the caps," Dr Brushem said.

He pointed to a diagram of a cap like Simon's, where just inside a microscopic chip would be inserted, re-creating the technology their fangs already possessed. By issuing these chips to children, Mrs Spinn was hoping their community (and soon, perhaps, the entire insect world!) could bypass the need for silk threads to connect to the World Wide Web. This could effectively eliminate WASP's hold on them.

"Here's how it works," he said, tapping the paperwork. "When someone comes in for a check-up, we'll give them a free cap in a special size to fit their species. It will connect to the internet when they get close enough to a webbook."

Dr Brushem paused and dug into his pocket. Once again, he wore his black leather jacket and boots and had his hair combed back with gel. He produced a prototype cap a lot like Simon's and gestured inside.

"It's a super small chip," he told them, "so nobody will know it exists."

"You mean, you're not going to tell people what the caps *really* do?"

The mosquito shook his head and grinned slyly. "It's a sccrct kept by the government at Westspinster. Life will continue as normal for a while until one of the silk threads is slashed or a virus is inserted by WASP. Then people will see they have an unexplainable, constant connection to the Web. Everyone can continue at work and school and not have to worry about interruptions and patches."

"And they'll never know *they* were the solution?" Dot gasped.

"*Uh-huh.*"

"I like it. I like it a LOT!" Dash said.

The dentist agreed but seemed prouder of their solution to the feud with WASP than he was guilty about deceiving people. Simon thought by the time anyone figured out the technology, the threat would be reduced and Dr Brushem and Claire Spinn would be heroes anyway. How could anyone get mad at them then?

"How are you going to be sure everyone wears a cap, though?" Dot asked. "Ours are real, but theirs have to be worn all the time, right?"

"At first we can only hope, but if enough people wear them around town, one cap will connect to another and another. As the trend takes off we think more and more young people will enjoy wearing them so proximity won't be a problem. They're not going to vibrate or glow as yours do; they'll look and feel like regular caps. "

Simon had an idea. "When people need new teeth or dentures, fillings or any other dental work, can't you fit something more permanent without them finding out? Then you're guaranteed to get enough people in town wearing them for the cap-to-cap connection!"

Dr Brushem held up his hand to high-five Simon, and they both chuckled.

"Smart lad," he said.

Simon blushed, though he assumed Dr Brushem and Mrs Spinn had already planned to do that in a few months.

"Why are you telling *us*, though?"

The mosquito wrung all his hands together and hummed.

Pacing, he said, "Well, Mrs Spinn and I have an important job for you."

"For *us*?" Dot gasped.

"*Uh-huh*." He raised an eyebrow in thought. "Are you interested?"

"Depends what it is," Dash said, crossing his legs and flicking through an old magazine. "What's in it for us?"

Simon knew they wouldn't be getting paid or rewarded for any of this, but he refrained from laughing at another of his friend's schemes.

"I've seen you admiring my snail," said Dr Brushem.

Dash suddenly looked up and threw his copy of Slug and Lettuce away. "Do *we* get one?"

The doctor cleared his throat, sorry to disappoint them. "Unfortunately, you're too young to legally ride a snail, but you'll get to meet the man who designed mine."

He paused, waiting for the children to cheer with delight.

Dash had other plans. "Is that *all*?"

"You drive a hard bargain," he said, "but all we need you to do, for now, is deliver our plans to *ScHnELL*. Alfrid Jennings—the owner—can make them in his workshop. He's a friend of ours."

Dr Brushem held out his hands and asked if they had a deal. Simon and Dot accepted immediately and promised not to tell their friends about the caps or the plans to stop WASP.

Dash was reluctant to agree to anything until he had a better reward.

The mosquito sighed and unfolded a sheet of paper containing samples of the new cap colours. He handed it to Dash and told him to choose his favourites.

"You can have as many as you want," he said. "That's my final offer."

Dash squealed and shook his hand. "You've got a deal!"

Chapter Nine

The Binary Twins skipped through the door to *ScHnELL* *w*hich was the workshop owned by Alfrid Jennings, a lime green aphid who had thick white hair and wore paint-covered grey overalls. Alfrid was in the shop managing his staff and he grinned when the children entered.

Most of the snails already in the shop were being spray-painted, but a few were up on platforms having some interesting accessories fitted. Simon saw: baskets, mudflaps, go faster eyebrows, flick down sunglasses, leather saddlebags, horns, tassels and padded seats (because a snail's shell could get very uncomfortable on your butt, especially on a long journey!). Some of the snails were having their shells waxed while others were being fitted with grips to prevent their riders from sliding off the back.

ScHnELL worked out of a large indoor garage, with open brick walls and a cold stone floor. It was dusty and paint-splattered and it smelled of unusual chemicals. An open metal door allowed passing snails to pull in for a check-up or an upgrade because Alfrid also offered them yearly health checks for road safety purposes. This made the workshop chilly and slimy in the winter.

The children were fascinated, pointing at various snails who were there to choose their designs. Dash saw one with a turquoise and purple tie dye pattern on the side, and Dot saw one with hearts and flowers painted over the entire shell; vibrant pink, yellow and orange on a cream background. Simon saw one painted like the night sky. It was completely jet black, decorated with tiny silver stars in various formations.

At the back in a small, sealed room, Dash waved to a freshly painted snail who was lying flat on a little blue towel. It was bright and hot as an oven in there, and the snail had to wear a pair of tiny black goggles to shield his eyes.

"You have *sunbeds* in here, too?" he asked one of the mechanics.

"Oh no," the mechanic chortled, "that's just how we dry the paint!"

Alfrid shook Dot's hand as he approached. "Willkommen, kinder!" he said.

"Danke," she replied, remembering her German lessons.

"What did he say?" Dash asked Simon when Alfrid turned his back.

Before Simon could answer, Dot interrupted and rolled her eyes. "He said 'welcome, children' and I thanked him because it's polite," she said, following Alfrid through the workshop.

Dash replied, "Oh, sorry, I took Spanish," then hurried along behind them.

Alfrid gave them a quick tour and introduced them to a few of his painters and mechanics, let them say hello (or 'Guten Tag' in German) to some of their regular customers and their riders, then took them to his office at the back. He locked the door and pulled down the blinds, then offered them a seat.

"Does everyone out there know, too?" Dash asked.

Alfrid shook his head. "Nein."

"*Nine* others know about the caps?" he gasped.

Dot leaned over and whispered, "No, Dash. Nein means no."

"Dr Brushem asked us to give you these," Simon said, handing him a copy of the dentist's documents. "Do you think you can make the chips?"

Alfrid grinned and said, "Ja."

"And that means yes," she confirmed.

"*I know what it means, Dot!*"

Alfrid was a man of few words but seemed pleased to help nevertheless. Simon handed him the remaining paperwork and watched as he fumbled for his monocle, fixing it against his eye. Then he dipped the tip of his nose in a glass of warm nectar.

"Ahhh!" he gasped and shuddered, allowing the sweet warm drink to chase away the chill.

"Do you know how long it will take to make them?" Dot asked.

"Uhm, a few weeks," he said with a heavy accent.

As Alfrid Jennings turned in his spinning chair to safely file the paperwork, Simon took the opportunity to nosey around the office.

It was a small space, crammed with oversized furniture (also covered in paint and grease) and large floor-to-ceiling filing cabinets. There was one door in and out and a square window. Simon thought he didn't really need blinds because you could smudge the dust on the glass with your finger. He did notice, however, an unusually placed bookshelf against the back wall; the width of a single door, stacked with somewhat irrelevant books. It looked a bit out of place.

On the top shelf were two books titled, *Reverend Mantis's Guide to Prayer* and, *There's a Louse in the House*.

On the second shelf were books called, *The Stylish Earwig's Guide to Wigs* and a catalogue called, *The 2018 Bed Bug Mattress Review*. There was even an old teen magazine titled, *How to Get a Kissing Bug to Kiss You*, which Simon *knew* didn't belong to Alfrid!

On the third shelf was a thick hardback called, *The Adventures of Cave Crickets*.

Simon had heard of them. They travelled the insect world, climbing mountains, braving rivers and venturing into underground tunnels. Simon had seen a few photographs on the walls of the workshop and one or two on Alfrid's desk of him with a bunch of other insects, all dressed in camouflage. He wondered if Alfrid had been in the military or if he was an ex-explorer, which would have explained at least *one* of his books.

Simon thought this was an unusual collection for an aphid of Alfrid's age. He nudged Dot and gestured silently at the books, who in turn elbowed Dash. Alfrid must've seen them exchanging whispers because he scowled at them.

Alfrid's monocle dropped suddenly onto the desk. "Ein problem?"

The Binary Twins gulped in unison.

"No, no, uhm, you like to read, Mr Jennings?" Simon said, trying not to feel intimidated.

For such a small insect, the way Alfrid manipulated his facial expressions made the three spiders feel insignificant and uneasy. Though the aphid's body was light and almost translucent in places, Simon had seen a skull and crossbones tattoo on his biceps (which were surprisingly defined) and even a piercing on his left antenna. It was clear Alfrid wasn't a pirate or a bandit, but Simon was sure he was more than a mechanic.

Why else would Mrs Spinn and Dr Brushem have sent them to the workshop?

"Ja," he replied, gruffly.

"Weird taste."

"Hmm." The aphid cracked his knuckles and snorted harshly, then gestured towards the door. "Time to go."

"But Dr Brushem hinted he might need our help again in future. If you tell us more then maybe—"

Through the accent, Simon struggled a little to make out his reply, but he was sure he said, "Brushem and Spinn will say when they are ready. Then we will talk."

Suddenly, the door behind them opened and in the frame appeared two large crane fly mechanics, neither of whom the children had met earlier. Compared to the spiders and especially to the aphid, they were huge and towered at least twice the height of the office door, meaning they had to crouch down and tuck in their wings to fill the space.

"This way," said one of the flies, using his long, spindly leg to hook the children and guide them out to the workshop. The children barely had the chance to check out some of the new customers' snails before he deposited them at the entrance and waited until they began to walk away.

Dot exhaled a sigh of relief when they had disappeared. "Who were *those* guys?"

"Looked like bodyguards to me," said Dash. "Jennings is a dodgy dude."

"I don't think he's dodgy," Simon told him, "but there's something strange. Did you see the books?"

Dot nodded and turned up her nose. "They were so dirty and torn; why hasn't he thrown those out?"

"I think they're a decoy for something," Simon said. "He doesn't strike me as being religious or interested in fashion."

Dash said, "Maybe you're right. I saw his tattoos. They were scary!"

"And faded, like they were done years and years ago."

"Maybe we should tell Dr Brushem what we saw?" Dot suggested.

The boys shook their heads and picked up the pace. They were already terrified of being followed home and beaten up by those crane flies.

Dash ran a finger across his throat. "No thanks, I'd like to live."

"Don't be so dramatic," said his sister, rolling her eyes. "How about you, Simon, what do you think we should do?"

Simon's legs were trembling. "Sorry, Dot."

They walked the rest of the way home in silence.

***

"We have to go into school, there's been a fire," said Mrs Ranchilla.

The children still had their coats and shoes on when she told them. They had only been home for a few minutes and weren't expecting to see Simon's mum in the hall. He was a bit worried she'd overheard them talking about *ScHnELL*.

"No more school *ever*!" he squealed.

"Your school's fine, but there's been an infestigation and the Head has called you in for a meeting."

"But we have two weeks off, and it's a weekend!" Simon protested. "We didn't do anything wrong, Mum."

His mother pulled on her jacket, scarf and boots while simultaneously opening the door, letting in the brisk winter breeze again. The children shuddered. They'd been looking forward to a cup of hot nectar and another mud pie.

"You're not in trouble," she promised. "It's got something to do with two grasshoppers in your class."

Dot asked, "Were their names Diddit and Ranoff? Did *they* set the fire?"

It was hard for the Binary Twins not to smile at the thought; finally, those bullies were getting what they deserved and justice would be served by the Head. Simon wasn't sure. Why would the Head want to speak to them if they hadn't been involved?

"That's what we're going to find out," she said. "I spoke to Mrs Spinn and she's heading there now."

She hurried the children out the door.

When they arrived, the damage to the school was obvious. The back of the building was black and grey and still smouldering in places. Prolice were guarding the scene, forming a barrier so nobody could get hurt. They said nothing to Simon and the others as they hurried through the main entrance and down the corridor to the Head's office.

Clive and Claire Spinn were already sat at his desk. They stood and hugged the twins when Mrs Ranchilla ushered everyone in.

"We didn't do anything wrong, honest," Dot told her parents.

"I'm sure this is a misunderstanding," said Clive.

The Head appeared in the doorway, prompting everyone to sit. The borer grub worm's huge round head was flushed and sweating, and although Simon was sure he'd done nothing wrong, the Head's lips were pulled back and his over-sized teeth were dominant, causing the children to sink down in their seats. Behind his rimless spectacles, the Head glared at his audience.

"Do you know two grasshoppers by the name of Diddit and Ranoff, Simon?"

Simon nodded. "They sit at the back of my history class, Head."

The Head slid a sheet of paper across the desk for Simon to read. He gasped when he realised it was a print out of the latest nasty eco-mail he'd received.

"Do you recognise that?" he asked.

Again, Simon nodded, a little embarrassed because his mum was in the room. Simon was pleased the Head knew about the bullying but wasn't sure how this connected to the fire.

The Head then slid a second sheet of paper across the desk towards the twins. It was a print out of the conversations they'd been having privately in class, using Dash's secret Binary code. But most of the words had been decoded, meaning the Head and their parents could read what had been said. Of course, there was nothing embarrassing or naughty in the documents because Simon, Dot and Dash were well behaved; they'd only chatted about homework, the prom and occasionally about the bullies, who they'd named a few times.

"Do you recognise that?" asked the Head.

Dash nodded and slid it to Dot, who blushed and said, "Yes, Head."

"You've been passing notes in class?" their mother asked, scowling.

Dot shrugged. "Dash developed our Binary system, Mum. It was the only way to talk without being picked on."

"You shouldn't be passing notes at all during lesson time," said Clive.

"It wasn't their fault," Simon admitted. "I asked Dash to make the code. Even in the corridors and the toilets, in the locker rooms and at lunch, they threaten us. Particularly me because of, well—" Simon smiled to reveal his blue fang. "I'm different."

"You *were* different," Dot told him. She smiled and reached over to hold his hand.

Simon was surprised. He thought he'd feel awkward or embarrassed holding a girl's hand in front of his best friend, her parents and the Head, but it wasn't weird at all. In fact, it felt quite natural and comfortable. Dot knew everything about him, including most of his secrets and fears because they spent a lot of time together. It made sense that she'd calm him down.

"We're sorry," Simon said. "It won't happen again, and I take full responsibility. Please don't punish my friends."

Mrs Ranchilla was about to ground Simon for the next two weeks (ruining his time off school and possibly even the prom) when the Head intervened.

"Punishment won't be necessary. We don't approve of you passing messages in class, but on this occasion, we're going to let it slide."

"Why would you do that?" asked Mrs Ranchilla, still frowning.

"Because Simon and his friends now have evidence against their bullies. It seems not only have they been upsetting your son, but also terrorising our night guard, Gary."

"Excuse me, Head, but how did you find out we were passing notes?" Dot asked quietly.

"They were eco-mailed to me anonymously, along with footage of the fire and various other documents." The Head slid a third sheet of paper across the desk, this time towards Clive and Claire. "Do you recognise this?"

The paper held two screen captures of profiles created on Scuttle Bugg, which could only have been accessed from a disc like the one she gave to Dash.

"Where's your copy of Scuttle Bugg?" Claire asked him.

Dash lowered his head. "They took it, Mum."

Clive's eyes widened. "Did they hurt you?"

"They put me in a headlock but I'm OK," he said. "Mrs Stinger intervened and they ran away, but they stole our lunch money and ruined our artwork."

Physically Dash has been unharmed, but he was ashamed they'd got the better of him in a public place. Spiders weren't as strong or muscly as grasshoppers and they couldn't fly; he'd been at a disadvantage, even with his friends' help.

"Sorry if I let you down, Dad," he said.

"You've done nothing wrong, Dash."

"Don't apologise," his mother said, slamming the sheet of paper on the desk in fury. "I want those grasshoppers excluded for their behaviour. Theft of my property is one thing, and setting fire to this school is another, but *nobody* hurts my kids and gets away with it!"

Dash beamed proudly at his mother. The twins had broken the rules and apologised; it felt good to be supported and praised for doing the right thing.

"We've already taken care of that, Mrs Spinn, I assure you," said the Head.

And they had. Not only had the grasshoppers had to face the Head at his worst, but the Prolice and Cockroach Infestation Department were now involved, too. The arsonists were being dealt with by the law. Hopefully, they'd learn their lesson!

"We also managed to salvage your disc, though I fear it was damaged by the fire." He retrieved a dirty, cracked disc from a shelf and handed it to Claire. "Whilst we haven't identified who sent these documents in, we'll be continuing to investigate over the holidays. For now, as a thank you for providing evidence, and an apology for your trouble, your tickets to the Winter Prom are complimentary."

Mrs Ranchilla smiled. "That's kind of you. The children are looking forward to it."

"Can we be assured this won't happen again?" Clive asked. "I'd hate to think other children are suffering, too."

"Absolutely," the Head said, then stood to shake their hands.

On his way out, Simon glanced back at the Head and offered his thanks with a pleasant smile.

The Head winked with one beady eye, then closed the door.

Chapter Ten

The children enjoyed their two weeks off school for the holidays and were able to relax and have fun. Mrs Spinn managed to convince the Head to allow Dot to join the prom's planning committee, and she was thrilled to be included. Her job was to decorate and organise the gymnasium. The committee had chosen a winter theme, with paper snowflakes, silver tinsel, lots of fake snow and white balloons strewn around the room. On each of the tables was a centrepiece surrounded by confetti, made from paper mache figurines and fake trees, and the napkins were all silver or white to match the bows on the chair backs.

Mrs Spinn took Dot shopping at the nearest mall for a beautiful frock; they'd tried on twenty different outfits, but finally, she chose a silky light pink dress which had a ribbon and lace along the bottom. Shoes for spiders could be very expensive (as they had to buy three pairs rather than one!), but thankfully, Dot already had some she liked. They were flat ballerina-style pumps in shimmering pink and were very comfortable to dance in.

Clive was so proud of Dash that he offered to buy the boys new tuxedos for their first prom night. While Dot was choosing her dress, Simon and Dash were in the tailors being measured for black trousers and matching jackets.

Simon agreed to take Dot to the prom after their meeting with the Head and thought it would be cool to match his tie to her dress, so Clive had to scurry across the mall to find out which one she'd bought.

Dash chose to wear a blue bow tie to match the cap he'd chosen at the dentist. Dr Brushem was right about the technology; he barely knew the chip was there and it had been easy to fit. Whilst he didn't have an official date for the prom, his friend Guy said they should go together as friends so they'd both have someone to dance with. Dash was excited to be going to the prom with Guy because he was a popular and handsome spider with thick black hair. Any photos they were in together would look smart. Though he was taller and chunkier than Dash, the two shared a sense of humour, so to mock Simon's choice to colour-coordinate with Dot, he and Guy were wearing matching bow ties too.

The gym was filling up quickly with excited children, all wearing their prettiest outfits. It was noisy and hot when Dash and Guy arrived. They headed straight for a drink of iced nectar and a look at the buffet, hoping to stuff their pockets with treats before the other kids got there first. The committee had planned to ensure there were plenty of mud pies, cookies, squirmy wormies and boiled sap sweets to go around, and they'd hired McFly's to cater the rest. Dash was excited to see Mega Mucks were on the menu!

The DJ was already playing lots of Dash's favourite songs, so it wasn't long before he and Guy were mingling with the other children, busting out their best moves to the Bee Onesies and the Beetles. He'd secretly been practising at home in front of the bedroom mirror. There were spinning disco balls fastened to the ceiling and cascading multi-coloured lights around the room, so it seemed much busier than it was.

But the chatter fell silent when Dot and Simon entered holding hands and smiling broadly, proud to show off their opposite blue fangs to the entire school. Some of the other insects (a few of them were now wearing coloured caps of their own!) gasped and pointed at the couple. Others whispered, 'Can you believe *their* fangs are real? It's so cool!' or 'We should go say hello to them', only to be held back by their starstruck friends.

Simon spotted all kinds of colours. Most of the girls had chosen pink or purple and lots of those were glittery, whereas the boys generally opted for blue or green. He was shocked to see Mrs Longlegs and Mrs Spinner were wearing one, too!

Dr Brushem was right! They were trendsetters; they were *popular*!

Dot suddenly froze and tugged Simon's hand when Diddit and Ranoff approached them through the crowd of dancing children. Their faces were emotionless at first as they carried plastic cups towards the couple, and Dot braced herself to be drenched in fruity spew. Instead, however, the grasshoppers offered Simon the drinks and smiled.

"We're sorry for what we did," said Ranoff.

Diddit offered Simon a friendly handshake and Dot tensed. There *had* to be a catch.

She locked her wide eyes on Dash across the dancefloor. He and Guy were ready to pounce. But to their surprise, the grasshoppers didn't seem to have a plan.

Simon accepted the handshake. "Uhm, thank you," he said. "Did you get into a lot of trouble?"

Diddit nodded. "Community service. We'll be breaking dung rocks in the quarry for a while, but the Head said we could come tonight if we wanted to apologise."

"So who *really* did it, then?" asked Dot.

Diddit scowled. "Did what, exactly?"

"Set fire to the school!"

"Oh, he did it," said Diddit.

"Is that true, Ranoff?" Simon asked.

"Probably not," Dot told him.

"No! I ran off," said Ranoff. "You did it, Diddit. I didn't do it."

"Did one do it while the other ran off? Or did you *both* do it and run off?" Dot asked.

"You can't run off while you're doing it, Ranoff. You did it and ran off after *I* ran off," Diddit said.

"How did *I* do it, Diddit? I ran off while you were doing it. I can't have done it if I ran off while *you* did it," said Ranoff. "So I didn't do it. Diddit did it. I ran off, and then Diddit did it and then ran off. Are we clear?"

Dot and Simon both tilted their heads, confused. In unison, they said, "Not really."

Simon added, "You were both there, so you both did it and ran off, Diddit and Ranoff!"

They all burst out laughing.

Then Ranoff sighed. "*Anyway*, we wanted to tell you we think your fangs are actually pretty cool. I guess we were just jealous."

The grasshoppers exchanged glances, excited to reveal their surprise and call a truce. They smiled together to reveal caps of their own. Simon was thrilled to see they'd chosen his favourite colour: BLUE!

"You can both come and hang out with us if you want, Simon," Diddit said, gesturing at another group of insects sitting over by the buffet.

"Sure," said Simon as he winked at Dot, "but my friends call me Bluetooth."

We hope you had FUN!

If you enjoyed reading this book and would like to support us further, there are lots of fun, free ways to do so! Here are some awesome ideas:

- Follow us on social media!
  - *Facebook.com/erachaelhardcastle*
  - *Instagram.com/erachaelhardcastle*
  - *Twitter.com/erhardcastle*
- Send us an eco-mail at:
  www.erachaelhardcastle.com
- Leave a review of the book on the World Wide Web! It's quick and easy to do.
- Post what you enjoyed most about our book on Scuttle Bugg (and any other social media platform) and be sure to tag us!
- Send us a photo of you reading the book with your family and friends. Remember to use our hashtags:
  - #bluetoothsavestheweb
  - #btwww
  - #scuttlebugg
- Tell your teachers what you learned by reading our book, and recommend us to your friends (human or insect!).
- Order our books at your favourite book store.

About The Authors

E Rachael Hardcastle is an Amazon International #1 bestselling author from Bradford, West Yorkshire. When she's not writing, Rachael helps other creatives around the world to write, edit and publish their books.

Rachael has a mission; she believes that writing helps us to face our fears and share important morals and values with others. She's passionate about community, too, and believes that through education we can inspire the next generation to do and create wonderful things.

Her dad, **David Hardcastle** also lives in Bradford (not far from Rachael—they go for lunch a lot!) and in their spare time, they like to think of other wacky stories to tell.

You can find out more about David and Rachael by visiting www.erachaelhardcastle.com, where you can join Rachael's tribe for regular updates, special offers and more!